'Don't set your sights on me.'

Bryn coolly studied Fleur's reaction to his words as he continued, 'I'm not on the marriage market.'

'I see. But I'm not on the marriage market either, so—' she smiled at him ruefully '—we might even find we get along like a house on fire, Mr Wallis.'

'Are you running away from a man, Fleur?'

'What makes you think that?'

Bryn shrugged. 'You must attract men like bees to a honeypot.'

Lindsay Armstrong was born in South Africa but now lives in Australia with her New Zealand-born husband and their five children. They have lived in nearly every state of Australia and tried their hand at some unusual, for them, occupations, such as farming and horse-training—all grist to the mill for a writer! Lindsay started writing romances when their youngest child began school and was left feeling at a loose end. She is still doing it and loving it.

Recent titles by the same author:

THE HIRED FIANCÉE
BY MARRIAGE DIVIDED
A QUESTION OF MARRIAGE

WIFE IN THE MAKING

BY
LINDSAY ARMSTRONG

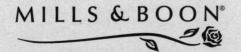

MILLS & BOON®

First published in Great Britain 2001
Harlequin Mills & Boon Limited,
Eton House, 18-24 Paradise Road, Richmond, Surrey TW9 1SR

© Lindsay Armstrong 2001

ISBN 0 263 82550 7

Set in Times Roman 10½ on 12 pt.
01-1101-48090

Printed and bound in Spain
by Litografia Rosés, S.A., Barcelona

CHAPTER ONE

FLEUR MILLAR studied the brief from the employment agency as she sat in the back of a taxi on her way to a Brisbane hotel for a job interview. One Bryn Wallis, restaurateur, was seeking a personal assistant cum bookkeeper who was also experienced with computers.

'Personal Assistant' was highlighted on the brief and there was a handwritten note that suggested a broad interpretation should be placed on this—'Be prepared to turn your hand to just about anything' was what the note said.

Fleur smiled fleetingly because she liked the sound of that—especially as the restaurant was situated on a tropical island. It would certainly make a change from being cooped up in an office as well as the rest of it. In fact, she realised, the prospect of this job had made her feel better and more positive than she had for a while...

The taxi deposited her and she made her way into the foyer of the luxury hotel and across to Reception, where she gave the name of the person she was to meet, and was personally—and more effusively than she would have expected—escorted by the concierge to a table in the adjacent lounge. The man sitting at it stood up with a frown as she approached and, rather distractedly, shook her proffered hand.

Early thirties, Fleur estimated, tall with a rangy, rugged physique that let you know he'd be quite capable of tossing you over his shoulder should he so desire—

to add you to his harem, for example—and the uncon-
ventional but interesting looks that made you wonder
whether you mightn't mind...

On the other hand, his clothes suggested very much
a man about town. He wore a pair of superfine bone-
cord trousers, a trendy cream linen shirt and a beautiful
and faultlessly-tailored tweed jacket. His hair was longish, a dark copper colour, his eyes were hazel, very
penetrating and not entirely approving, she couldn't
help feeling, and his hand was lean and strong.

So, mixed signals, she thought. Damn! Why couldn't
he have been a more conventional restaurateur? But she
immediately countered this thought with the wry re-
flection that there was probably no such thing, as well
as a caution not to judge on appearances, and sat down
to smile across at him, unable to hide her eagerness to
get this job.

Bryn Wallis shoved a hand through his tawny hair and
stared grimly at the girl sitting opposite him so hopefully. She was gorgeous, having stunning, long-lashed
deep blue eyes, a river of smooth, bluntly cut, medium
blonde hair that fell loose from a side parting to below
her shoulders, a wide brow tapering to a beautifully
defined jaw line and the most elegant, fastidious nose.

Her perfection didn't end there, either. Her whole
aura was elegant although her clothes were simple. She
wore well-pressed, tailored jeans, a white shirt and a
navy jacket. But beneath was a shapely body and long
legs—she was about five feet six, he judged—and a
graceful mover with slim expressive hands, although—
the only fault he could find—she bit her nails.

She was also not a day over twenty, if he was any
judge, which meant all sorts of things but principally

that he could end up feeling responsible for her and that would be counterproductive, since he'd been down that road before and because he was looking for someone to share *his* responsibilities.

He sighed savagely. 'What the hell am I going to do with you—uh—' he glanced at the paperwork in front of him to discover that she was aptly named '—Fleur?'

She put a thumb to her mouth as if to bite the nail then stopped herself and twisted her hands together. 'I gather I'm not what you expected, Mr Wallis?'

'Not in the least. That is to say,' he sought to sweeten that blunt statement then shrugged and decided to opt for honesty, 'you're far too young and inexperienced, you would be the kind of distraction I need like a hole in the head and I don't think you'd be tough enough.'

She thought through this quite calmly, which surprised him a bit, but she surprised him even more when she said with a slight smile, 'I don't know why but people do tend to take me for younger when in fact I'm twenty-three.'

He blinked then frowned down at the paperwork, to have this fact confirmed. 'All the same—' he started to say.

'No, although I have a degree, I'm not terribly experienced in the workplace,' she agreed, 'but you will find a couple of good references amongst my résumé and you'd be very welcome to check them out.'

This time he flicked through the paperwork to see that she did indeed have a degree in computer science and business applications, with honours, what was more. And the two references, which he scanned swiftly, were impressive.

'I'm not quite sure what you mean by a distraction,'

she went on, with—could it have been a secret little gleam of laughter in those stunning eyes? he wondered, 'but perhaps I should reassure you that I never,' she paused for emphasis, 'mix business with pleasure.'

Bryn Wallis knew he was doing it but couldn't help himself—he smiled coolly and cynically.

She said nothing but looked him straight in the eye, all secret amusement gone from hers now so that it was a particularly level gaze he found himself returning.

Well, well, Miss Fleur, he thought and, for the first time since the employment agency had presented him with this highly unsuitable candidate, felt intrigued.

'And,' she said, 'I'm not sure why I would need to be for personal assistant duties and to work a computer, but I'm as strong as a horse, Mr Wallis.'

'I meant mentally tough, Ms...?' He found he couldn't remember her surname.

'Millar,' she supplied flatly. 'Fleur Millar, with an A.'

It was the second tinge of acerbity he'd detected, a sign that he might be getting under the gorgeous Miss Millar's skin, Bryn mused and decided he enjoyed doing that for some odd reason...

So he went on with a certain amount of relish, 'I'm not easy to work with, I can be impatient, scathing, intolerant and the last thing I need is a girl who will dissolve into tears when the going gets rough.' He waited but she made no comment other than narrowing those blue eyes slightly.

'What's more,' he continued, 'since this is a live-in position on an island, you wouldn't be able to go home to Mum every evening, out to the movies or whatever, to slough all that off.'

'It's not a permanent position, though,' she pointed

out. 'I was given to understand the duration was three months. That's not very long.'

He grimaced. 'Long enough to have a gutful of me, Fleur. The other thing is, it's not only straight PA,' he gestured impatiently, 'office duties I had in mind, so you could in fact be *over-qualified* for the position.' He paused and congratulated himself on thinking of that.

'I,' he went on, 'need someone who is prepared to muck in and be a receptionist, wait tables, play cricket with my kid when I don't have the time—even peel potatoes should I be short-staffed. I need a bloke in other words.' Once more Bryn Wallis shoved his hand through his hair. 'That's why I asked the agency not for a *Girl* Friday but a Man Friday,' he added bitterly.

Fleur raised her eyebrows. 'I don't think you're allowed to do that in this day and age, Mr Wallis. Discriminate on the basis of sex. And it so happens that while I'm not much good at cricket, I do play a mean game of chess, I like children and…I can peel potatoes as well as any man.'

He paused and their gazes clashed.

'I also gather,' she said after a long, fraught moment, 'that your bookwork is in a bit of a mess. I've recently specialized in a computer program that I could install and run for you, so it could all be done electronically and correctly and I'd be happy to show you how to work it.'

Bryn lay back in his chair and looked around the plush Brisbane hotel lounge he was conducting this interview in at the same time as he pondered how deceptive appearances could be. This girl, who had started out looking vulnerable and hopeful as well as potential Hollywood starlet material, was beginning to exhibit a mind like a steel trap.

Perhaps his less than tactful approach had crushed that hopeful air he'd divined, or perhaps he'd imagined it—not that it mattered, he still didn't want her for the job, but…

'Why do you want to bury yourself on an island for three months, anyway?' he asked abruptly.

He saw the momentary hesitation in her eyes before she looked away, and said quietly, 'I thought it would be a nice change from working in an office, in a high-rise building, in a city.'

Yes, and all the rest you don't want to tell me, Miss Millar, he reflected sardonically. 'Incidentally,' he said, '*I* don't believe in mixing business with pleasure either. But it'd be fair to say you *would* provide a distraction I need like a hole in the head.'

Her gaze came back to him. 'Why?'

He looked her up and down from head to toe ironically. 'Hedge Island,' he said, 'does not have a large population but we recently acquired an upmarket resort situated on the other side of the island from Clam Cove, where I am. This has been a boon for my restaurant,' he said rather shortly, 'because guests of the resort patronize me when they feel like a change of scene, not to mention stunning food.'

'So?' Fleur enquired politely.

'I don't know if you're familiar with the workings of upmarket island resorts—'

'It so happens I am,' she said coolly.

He chewed his lip and studied her. 'Well, then,' he drawled, 'you probably don't need me to tell you that their water-sports department alone employs at least six lusty, good-looking young men who are cut off from their sweethearts or whatever. Then there's the golf instructor, the tennis coach, the pilots, the guests themselves and so on. Thus,' he said, 'it could become a full-time job helping you to fend off unwelcome advances.' He eyed her sardonically. 'Not to mention the possibility of you being poached away from my job.'

'I can do my own fending off, thank you, and I have no intention of being poached. On the other hand,' she said thoughtfully, 'if my presence were to bring in more customers, could that be a bad thing, Mr Wallis?'

Getting more and more like a steel trap by the moment, Bryn mused unamusedly. 'You might be right,' he replied with a glint of satire in his hazel eyes. 'Both on the customer issue and because I think you might also be a smart...be smart enough to look after yourself.'

'Thank you,' she said, serenely ignoring his heavily sarcastic tone and what he patently hadn't said. 'When would you like me to start?'

'Oh, no, you don't, Miss Millar. I haven't agreed to anything yet because even if we dismiss your looks—please don't think I mean to be uncomplimentary about them incidentally but—'

'Forgive me for doubting you, Mr Wallis,' she broke in swiftly, 'but I do. I seem to have put your hackles up from the moment you laid eyes on me. What puzzles me is why, at the same time, you should be attributing these...' she gestured '...these...Helen of Troy powers to me? One would have thought it was quite a contradiction.' She gazed at him questioningly then added composedly, 'Other than that, I'm quite sure I could cope with the job. But, naturally, it's up to you.'

Somewhat to his amazement, Bryn heard himself saying, 'It's *isolated* unless you want to hang around the resort. If you're not attuned to the life, it can be boring. Getting to the mainland, to hairdressers, beauty parlours, the movies and the like on your days off takes an hour boat ride each way and I'm told boats are most conducive to bad hair days anyway.'

She merely looked at him with that secret amusement again.

'All right. There is one last embargo, Fleur Millar.' He studied her coolly. 'Don't set your sights on me.'

Whether it was his bluntness or the subject itself, he couldn't say, but those blue eyes definitely widened in surprise. And she seemed genuinely lost for words.

Then she made a rolling motion with her slim hands as she said, 'You…have a problem with that?'

'I have a problem with that,' he agreed ironically. 'But I'm not on the marriage market.'

'I see. Well,' she enlarged and summed him up from head to toe, 'it's not hard to see why—you have the problem, I mean.'

'Thank you,' he returned, grimly polite.

'But I'm not on the marriage market either, so,' she smiled at him ruefully, 'we might even find we get along like a house on fire, Mr Wallis.'

He let about half a minute pass in silence, then, 'Are you running away from a man, Fleur?'

'What makes you think that?'

He didn't answer immediately because he'd noted that momentary hesitation again. Then he shrugged. 'A girl with your undoubted intelligence despite your looks should know why I'm wondering that, Fleur. You must attract men like bees to a honey pot.'

He saw the shutters come down in her eyes, and noted the way her gorgeous mouth trembled slightly. But she stood up and said evenly enough, 'Keep your job, Mr Wallis. I'll find something else.'

He stood up too. 'Sorry—that was unnecessary. If you want it, it's yours.'

Her eyes widened. 'What made you change your mind?'

Heaven alone knows, Bryn Wallis thought drily; I can feel in my bones that I'm going to regret this! He said, however, and smiled crookedly, 'I'm desperate.'

Three weeks later Fleur walked along a sandy beach that fringed a turquoise bay between steep, wooded headlands to her tiny bungalow on Hedge Island.

There were three accommodation bungalows set wide apart next to the beach. The largest was inhabited by Bryn Wallis and his son, and a slightly larger version of her own was currently occupied by the only other live-in restaurant staff, Julene and Eric Philips, who were taking a break from sailing around the world to earn some money.

Julene was assistant chef although that was another job description worthy of a broad interpretation. And Eric, who was a giant of a man with bleached blond hair that made you think of a Viking reincarnated, was very much a jack-of-all-trades, who could turn his hand to just about anything—bar keeping the books. In contrast to his wife, he said very little. All other staff were locals who lived on the island.

Although her bungalow was the essence of simplicity with a palm-thatch roof and similar windows that you propped open, it was sturdily built, and had its own modern bathroom. It also afforded her absolute privacy and the veranda, complete with hammock, had stunning views over the bay.

In fact she often felt like a castaway not on a desert island but in a tropical paradise. There was the beach and some coral reefs at the mouth of the bay which were wonderful to snorkel over and also protected the bay. There were the headlands, covered in bush and studded with tall, dark green hoop pines and grey boulders, and she loved to watch the fish hawks and brahminy kites that soared from their nests through the sky with their high, clear whistles. There were cockatoos and rosellas, pigeons and plovers and often, at night, the mournful cry of curlews.

Behind the beach and around the buildings that fitted in with the landscape so well, a riot of colour had been created. Bougainvillaea, in many shades, the yellow trumpet flowers of the allamanda creeper, frangipani and hibiscus as well as native grevilleas, bottle brush and melaleucas, coral trees and impatiens.

All of it appealed not only to her senses but suited her mood and her simple needs of the moment. Not only that, she reflected and rubbed her neck wearily as she walked up the steps, the beauty of Clam Cove formed her retreat from the impossible demands of Bryn Wallis.

She poured herself a cool drink and slipped into the hammock. He was every bit as bad as he'd painted himself—sarcastic, arrogant, impatient and volatile. Added to all that, she'd divined that, although he loved to cook, not far beneath the surface there were times when he not only loathed to cook for the public but he loathed having to share his bit of tropical paradise with them.

So why, she wondered not for the first time, was he doing it?

But Bryn Wallis was a mystery in many respects. His son, Tom, six, was a delightful bundle of energy and mischief as well as extremely bright, and she and

Tom had formed an instant rapport because he was wild to learn about computers and have someone to play computer games with. But, while it was patently obvious that Tom didn't have a mother around, there was no explanation of what might have happened to her. Tom never spoke of her.

Fleur had found out that they'd lived on Hedge Island for some time and that the restaurant was only open during the cooler winter months. Although other people lived on the island, the population was small and, although people came to the island all year round, it was the winter influx of southern visitors, visitors escaping the rigours of colder winters down south for the still balmy warmth of the north, that made it viable.

All in all, she thought, Bryn Wallis came across as a man who had decided to opt out of the rat race, but the reason for it was another matter. There was no sign at Clam Cove, which was the name of his restaurant as well as his little slice of paradise, that he'd ever been anything else but a beachcomber who loved to dive, swim, fish, cook when the mood was on him, and turn his hand to building bungalows and making some exquisite pieces of wooden furniture.

Although she did wonder sometimes if he was a writer because of something Tom had said, and because, some nights when she couldn't sleep, often the early hours of the morning she'd noticed a lamp on in the main bungalow.

He was also a man of decided opinions and causes. In two and a half weeks she'd heard him declaim scathingly on the iniquities of longline fishing and the declining albatross and dolphin population and conversely on the protection of crocodiles to the extent that the creatures could now be found in Cairns, their near-

est coastal city, itself. She'd been subjected to his ve-
hemence on genetic food engineering and discovered
that he had a thing about women who wore artificial
nails.

It had amused her to think that was probably the only
thing he approved of about her.

As for the restaurant itself, it had soaring palm-
thatch ceilings, was open-sided with roll-down clear
plastic blinds in case of inclement weather, and was
built over the beach. It featured his pieces of furniture,
some wonderful pottery urns planted with flowering
plants and creepers, as well as nautical and beachcomber memorabilia hung from the rafters.

There was no separate cooking area. The chef op-
erated from a raised, counter-enclosed area where Bryn
did a lot of his cooking on rotisserie spits and grids
over charcoal fires. On starry, moonlit nights with the
water lapping close by it was especially exotic and romantic.

One mystery she had solved, though, was why he
might not be on the marriage market.

The deputy manager of the resort on the other side
of the island was a woman, Stella Sinclair, a very attractive brunette in her early thirties. Although she
blended in with the tropical ambience of the island
well, Fleur had detected a sharp brain and consummate
businesswoman in Stella Sinclair. And Julene, who was
something of a character, had let slip to Fleur that,
although on account of Tom it was never alluded to at
Clam Cove, the rest of the island well knew that Stella
was Bryn Wallis's lover.

But the most puzzling aspect of all about the man,
Fleur reflected, was his deep and instant antipathy to
her. Yes, no one around him got a smooth ride when

the restaurant was busy and things went wrong even if they were not the culprit. But they put up with it because at other times he could be charming, funny, kind even and irresistible. His son adored him and he seemed to have a natural way with the boy.

They were often to be seen working together, which meant that Tom fetched and carried tools for Bryn as he did some woodwork. They were often to be heard having long, serious conversations about anything and everything then breaking up into laughter or song. And Tom cherished the growing menagerie of little animals Bryn carved for him.

Not so with her, however. He had a subtle way of needling her, he was a genius at innuendo and the kind of *double entendre* that might float over other heads but found their mark with her unerringly like well-placed arrows intended to wound. There was an undoubted and barely veiled hostility in all his dealings with her even though, so far, she'd not retaliated in kind. Why? she wondered, staring out to sea unseeingly.

In the two and a half weeks since she'd started working for him she'd gone out of her way not to put a foot wrong. She'd 'turned her hand' to everything that was requested of her, including all the things he himself had mentioned bar cricket. But she'd more than compensated for that by spending as much time with Tom as she could when Bryn wasn't able to. This had been no hardship. Tom was a real character and exceptionally articulate for his age.

And she'd gone out of her way, when helping out in the restaurant, to attract as little attention as possible. She'd scraped her hair back, worn no make-up and a dowdy, voluminous dress she'd had the forethought to purchase before arriving on the island. Not only that, but to date she hadn't set foot beyond Clam Cove.

Also, while she'd been meticulous as a waitress or the receptionist, she'd also been at pains not to allow her natural sense of fun or anything that could be termed *joie de vivre*, come-hitherness or whatever it was Helen of Troy might have possessed, to show through.

True, there had still been some speculative glances but to say that she was providing the kind of distraction he needed like a hole in the head was simply not true. Unless...

No, she thought. No. She couldn't be distracting *him*. There was absolutely no sign of it, he had Stella... No.

In fact, he had Stella at that moment, although quite properly, she realized as her gaze focused over the veranda. The deputy manager of the resort had come for lunch and was now strolling along the beach with Tom and Bryn. They all wore their swimming costumes, and as Fleur watched they plunged into the sea and started to splash each other.

She watched for a while, unable to control a desolate little sense of envy. They looked like a family engaged in such simple fun and togetherness. Stella wore a red bikini and Bryn a faded pair of green board shorts. In fact, board shorts, an old frayed straw hat and a shark's tooth on a leather thong around his neck was his preferred mode of dress on the island. Nor did his preferred mode of dress on the island do much to conceal a rather breathtaking physique.

Not that she hadn't suspected it at the interview in Brisbane but it had come as a bit of a shock to see him like this after his sartorial elegance that day. Nor had the way he'd been dressed at the interview given her to suspect that when in Clam Cove restaurant mode, as opposed to beachcomber mode, he would wear a red bandanna around his longish tawny hair, black trousers and a white pirate shirt with an emerald cummerbund.

The first time she'd seen him thus arrayed she'd been tempted to laugh, but had desisted on receiving a laser-like glance from those hazel eyes that seemed to promise she could be made to walk the plank should she exhibit any amusement.

Strangely enough she soon realized that, although the surprise of it had been amusing, she was not alone in finding him oddly magnificent in this get-up. Many a woman guest followed him around with their eyes. Especially on those starry, romantic nights. Were they visualising being tossed over his shoulder and carried off to be made love to in a way that his physique and sheer, magnetic arrogance made promise of an experience never to be forgotten?

She stirred in the hammock as she watched Bryn Wallis stand in the shallows with his hands planted on his hips, with his back to the beach, as he watched Stella and Tom race towards him, and felt an odd little contraction at the pit of her stomach that reinforced the fear she had that she might be no different from some of his restaurant guests...

So, she thought, he wasn't being impossibly egotistical when he said he had a problem with women. Damn. And she turned to her other side restlessly and closed her eyes determinedly. Remember, Fleur, she told herself, no more men...

A week later, the day started out like any other.

She went for an early morning swim, alone. She had a simple breakfast of fruit and muesli with Tom and

Julene. Eric was out fishing, it appeared, but of Bryn there was no sign until Tom explained why.

'Bryn didn't get back from the resort last night—I wonder why?' Tom had the habit of calling his father by his first name, which always made Fleur want to smile. But there was no doubting whose child he was—he had fair hair but his father's hazel eyes, and not only that; although only six, he also had his father's, when Bryn chose to be that way, charm and wit.

Julene removed Tom's empty plate and said soothingly, 'That's why you spent the night with us, honey, remember? In case it got too late for your dad to come home. I expect he'll be here any time soon!'

'I hope it's before I go to school!' Tom said enthusiastically.

'I guarantee he'll be here when you get home after school!' Julene promised. 'And, talking of school, you've got five minutes before the bus arrives! Off you go—and don't forget your lunch,' she added, pointing to a plastic box on the counter.

Tom went, scooping up his lunch on his way past.

Julene subsided and poured herself another cup of coffee to which she appeared to be addicted. She was an easy-going, friendly, bottle-blonde in her late thirties who loved nothing better than a good chat and displaying her voluptuous figure in a series of vibrantly coloured sarongs that made Fleur feel dull by comparison in her sensible shorts and T-shirts.

Now she grimaced as she sipped her coffee. 'I'd say *la* Stella is putting on an act. Although we often babysit Tom for him, he doesn't usually stay overnight.'

Fleur gazed at her. 'What kind of an act? They always seem so...relaxed and well-suited when she's here.'

'I'm sure that's what she thinks,' Julene commented, 'which is why it's probably a puzzle to her that she's not getting any further forward with our Bryn.'

'As in…?'

'As in nailing him, honey, trotting him down the aisle, getting a ring on her finger,' Julene explained laconically. 'The man is dynamite, in case you hadn't noticed.' This time she frowned at Fleur.

Fleur shrugged, decided that denying it would give cause for curiosity if not be a waste of time, and said laconically back, 'Yep. But I got the impression she was a career woman and, well…' She paused.

'That's the effect Bryn has! Lord knows even I wasn't immune at first.'

Fleur blinked. 'But you and Eric are such an ideal couple.'

'We still are. It doesn't stop you from looking over the fence occasionally and,' she spread her hands and laughed infectiously, 'wondering, now, does it, doll?' she added.

'I've never been married,' Fleur replied with a glint of laughter in her eyes. 'But I don't think it would do me the slightest good to wonder too much about Bryn. In case *you* hadn't noticed, he treats me as if I've crawled out from under a stone.'

Julene sobered. 'I must say, you could have knocked us over with a feather when he produced you, Fleur. Still, I guess he had his reasons!' She got up and began to collect the dishes.

'He did. He was desperate.' Fleur rose and helped her clear the table. 'Mind you, I can see why. His book-work is chaotic. It's going to take me all of the three months to sort it out and his last tax return has been queried. Strange,' she said more to herself than Julene, 'you wouldn't think he'd be that, I guess, uninterested in his own affairs.'

Julene was silent and when Fleur looked at her it appeared as if the other woman was debating with herself. She even opened her mouth, closed it, then said simply, 'Takes all kinds, doll! Don't you worry about the dishes!' and departed for the washing-up area round the back of the restaurant.

Fleur hesitated with the feeling she'd had a door closed in her face, then neatly stacked the salt and pepper shakers on the rack, shook out the tablecloth—and went to her office.

"Office" was a misnomer.

She had a small room also off the back of the restaurant with one table, one chair, a computer, yes, but no drawers, no filing cabinets—none of the normal office furniture in fact. Bryn's preferred system of filing had been nails in the wall onto which he affixed his paperwork, but by no means all of it. The rest of it had overflowed across every available inch of table surface. And the computer had obviously just come out of the box but not even been connected yet.

She'd drawn a deep breath on being introduced to her office, had turned to Bryn Wallis to protest that no one could be expected to work like this—but had changed her mind suddenly. Because he'd been watching her with the obvious and cynical expectation of her making a fuss and more than that, a certain relish at being able to point out to her she *was* unequal to this particular job.

An extremely unladylike piece of advice for him had crossed her mind but she'd managed not to say it.

She'd merely shrugged and turned back to the computer.

'Good enough for you, Ms Millar?' he'd enquired.

'More than good enough.' She'd paged through the literature. 'You have enough memory here to store the workings of a worldwide chain of restaurants but I always say better to have too much than too little—memory, that is. I'll need a screwdriver, Mr Wallis. Do you intend to get an e-mail address for the restaurant, incidentally?'

'That was the idea. Can you handle the setting up of it, Miss Millar?' he'd replied, stressing the AR at the end of her surname.

'I can; I see you have an internal modem but I need a phone line in here.' She'd looked around.

'*Voilà*—I'm not quite as useless about all this as you imagine,' he'd drawled and picked up a stack of papers to reveal a phone. 'Not only did I get this phone installed but it is also on a separate line.'

'Good thinking,' she'd murmured coolly. 'Uh—would there be anything resembling stationery?'

He'd subjected her to a lengthy aren't-you-a-clever-little-miss? gaze then strolled across the room and hefted a cardboard box onto the tables. 'Pads, pens, paper for the printer, envelopes—I even got stamps.'

'How thoughtful,' she'd commented.

Their gazes had clashed then he'd smiled sweetly. 'Thank you—well, I'll leave you to it, Fleur.' And he'd walked out.

She'd gritted her teeth and restrained herself from throwing something at him. But she'd reminded herself that she'd almost always known this would be a challenge and now was not the time to get faint-hearted. By that evening, with Eric's help—he'd provided her with some boxes she could use as file boxes and rustled up another table—she'd been more or less up and running, even able to play computer games with Tom.

It was Tom who'd, at the same time, told her that Bryn had a laptop computer in their bungalow but never seemed to have the time to play computer games with him.

'So—what does he do on it?' she'd asked, taken by surprise because she'd formed the impression her boss was computer illiterate.

'He just writes things, that's all. Oh, wow! We've got that new computer game, Fleur. Let's play that!'

But, she reflected, coming back to the present as she looked around her 'office', three and a half weeks of utter professionalism and making the best of things without one murmur of discontent had obviously not changed Bryn Wallis's view, whatever it was, of her.

She pulled her chair out and sat down but, for perhaps a good five minutes, stared unseeingly at the wall with a frown in her eyes. Then she shrugged and switched on the computer.

At five o'clock that same evening the day was starting to assume catastrophic proportions. Julene took to her bed with a migraine. Lobster, a great favourite on the Clam Cove menu, had to be struck off because the outboard motor on the dinghy, the only dinghy used to catch the lobster fresh every day from the waters around the island, seized up and required a part to be sent from the mainland, something that could take a day. Tom came home from school feeling feverish and uncomfortable, and with the news that his best friend had chickenpox.

Fortunately the reservation list for dinner was small; on the other hand only one waitress from Bryn's list of casual local staff had been rostered on and she called in late afternoon to report that she'd just sprained her ankle. Frantic telephoning around had not produced a replacement for her although Bryn had enlisted the aid of the community nurse to sit with Tom.

It was when he'd exhausted all possibilities of getting anyone to replace Julene or the waitress that Bryn slammed the phone down and said savagely to Fleur, 'Let's see how you cope with this, Miss Competence Personified!'

'Just you and me?' she hazarded.

'Eric can help wait tables,' he said shortly and eyed her sardonically. 'Are you on?'

'Of course,' she replied calmly.

Five hours later, the last guests had departed, the candles were guttering in their glasses and the cooking area was a scene of colourful chaos.

Fleur looked around at the tables that needed to be cleared, at the huge, decorative bowl of fruit on the counter. Her gaze drifted on over the dirty sauce pots in which fragrant, pastel and delicious sauces had been prepared, the lined-up empty bottles of wine, and paused as she spotted one that was not empty—a half-full bottle of Chianti in fact.

Whereupon she ceremoniously removed her apron, reached for a glass and poured some of the wine, then turned to her boss, who was looking at her quizzically, and threw the Chianti into his face.

'Take that,' she spat at him. 'I have never in my life witnessed such an exhibition of boorish behaviour or been treated so shockingly when all I was trying to do was help! Not only trying, incidentally, but it's only thanks to me that they didn't all get up and walk out!'

Bryn blinked several times and wiped his eyes. 'I was under a bit of pressure,' he started to say, 'which I'm the first to admit can affect me adversely—'

'Rubbish!' she yelled at him. 'You deliberately set out to make this evening as difficult as possible for me with your cutting little remarks, your dreadful impatience, your insolent looks and all the rest. You deliberately set out to get me as flustered as possible—just as you have been ever since we set eyes on one another. Well, here's what I think of you, Bryn Wallis!' This time it was a bowl of unwhipped cream she poured over him.

And when he started to laugh, she upended another bowl down the front of his clothes—a bowl of raspberries. But as she turned to find something else to pour over him, he simply picked her up and carried her, kicking and fighting, down the stairs to the beach, where he walked straight into the sea with her.

CHAPTER TWO

'PUT me down!' Fleur ordered and pummelled Bryn ineffectually.

He did so, up to her knees in water, but kept his hands around her waist.

'Now let me go!' she gasped, unable to believe what was happening to her as her skirt billowed wetly around her legs. 'I don't know who you think you are or what you think you're doing, but this is *crazy*.'

She looked around wildly but Clam Cove was serene with its curve of white beach fringed by shadowy palm trees. There were no lights on in any of the cottages, although the restaurant was still lit, there was no sign of Eric, and beneath the surface of the water her shoes sank into the sand.

'Fleur,' he said mildly, 'you're almost as messy as I am.'

She glanced down at herself then up to the heavens in furious exasperation because she was also now liberally coated with cream and raspberries.

'Therefore,' he continued reasonably, 'I thought we both might avail ourselves of the sea's cleansing properties.' And, so saying, he lifted her off her feet and moved to deeper water so that when he put her down again, it lapped around her shoulders and was about mid-chest height for him, but still he didn't release her waist.

And he actually smiled down at her as he said,

'Now, that's not so bad, is it? A bit cool but then we were both overheated—emotionally at least.'

But Fleur was not ready to be placated in any way. 'Cool?' she retorted with her teeth chattering. 'I'm freezing and you're mad, Bryn Wallis! Not only mad but horrible and…and…'

As her voice broke he released her waist but took her hand. 'Can you float on your back, Fleur?'

'Of course I can float on my back but it's not something I usually do fully clothed and with my shoes on in the middle of the night!' she replied witheringly.

'Take them off and give it a try,' he suggested. 'The Southern Cross is up there bright and clear—it's a marvellous way to do a bit of star-gazing.' He let her hand go and pulled off his bandanna then his shirt and tossed them away from him.

'If you're suggesting,' she said arctically, 'that I—'

'Just down to your undies,' he reassured her and, not without some difficulty, pulled his trousers off under the water and threw them away too. 'Feels wonderful!' Two shoes and a pair of socks bobbed away from them. 'And I'm still quite decent, believe me.' He lay back to reveal a pair of boxer shorts and, with his ankles crossed, floated gently and with little effort. 'The more you're in it, the warmer it gets incidentally,' he told her seriously. 'Wow, just saw a falling star!'

Fleur muttered something and, with no real idea why she was doing it other than that she felt awful with her voluminous dress clinging to her and weighing her down, struggled out of it and threw it away from her. To her surprise, she was immediately conscious of a sense of liberation mental as well as physical. So she reached for her shoes and consigned them to sink or swim, and dived beneath the water. When she surfaced she dragged her hair out of her eyes and flipped onto her back to float as effortlessly as did her tormentor.

There was a sheen of starlight on the dark surface of the water, and the soft, rhythmic sound of waves breaking on the reef that protected Clam Cove. The Milky Way looked like silver tinsel pasted to a midnight-blue heaven, so close you felt you could reach out and touch it.

'Not such a bad idea after all?' he suggested.

'I still think you're quite mad,' she replied after a long moment. 'Nor have I forgiven you for anything, but…the stars are fantastic.'

He laughed softly. 'You were fantastic tonight as a matter of fact.'

Fleur sank beneath the surface and came up spluttering. 'So why…?'

'Race you to the beach, and after I've made you a nightcap I'll tell you.'

'No—'

'Fleur, lovely as this is, enough is enough.' He flipped over. 'Ready?'

'I…oh, all right!'

They reached the beach together and he took her hand as they waded out of the water. 'Let's run,' he suggested. 'Just to your bungalow.'

'Hang on—what other Olympic endeavours do you have in mind for me tonight?' she enquired a little bitterly.

'None,' he assured her, 'but it will ward off the cold.'

She hesitated then remembered she was standing before him in her bra and briefs. Indeed, as she hesitated his gaze slid up and down her sleek wet body and a *frisson* communicated itself to her to be beneath his gaze wearing only a mostly lace bra and a triangle of matching satin and lace, both pasted to her skin revealingly... Had it come from him through their hands? she wondered. Or was it only she who was responding, not only to her state of undress but also to Bryn Wallis, who was tall and rangy and rather magnificent?

She shook her head to dispel these thoughts and said with some acerbity, 'OK, but that's my last form of exercise for the night!'

He grinned and they started to jog down the beach towards her bungalow.

Twenty minutes later she'd showered and was wrapped in an ice-blue towelling robe and drying her hair, when he returned bearing a tray. He came into the bungalow wearing an old football jersey with cut-off sleeves and a pair of khaki shorts, with his tawny hair ruffled and spiky as if he'd dragged a towel through it then used his fingers as a comb. And he had on the tray two of the house specials—Irish coffee à la Clam Cove in tall glasses with filigree silver holders, topped with swirled cream and sprinkled with chocolate.

She raised an eyebrow but didn't comment and sat down on the bed beneath the furled-up mosquito net so he could have the only chair. In typical Bryn Wallis fashion, however, which was to say there was never any disputing who owned and ran the place if not to say dominated it, he made a few adjustments to the room before he sat down. He lit the oil lamp she never used because he'd explained to her it was only for power failures, and switched off the overhead light. Then he adjusted the pole that lowered the palm-frond window so that it was only open a few inches.

Finally, he looked around and commented that she needed another chair.

Fleur lowered the towel she was using to dry her hair and replied that she wasn't planning to entertain anyone in her bungalow on a regular basis so one chair was fine with her.

'Yes, well,' he said a little drily and brought her coffee over to her, 'perhaps you should.'

Her eyes widened, then she smiled ironically. 'You were the one who was afraid of just that,' she reminded him.

He studied her comprehensively, her fresh, perfect, radiant skin, the fair silk of her drying hair, the elegance of her chin, her slender neck enfolded in the blue terry towelling and the twisted grace of her body as she sat sideways on the edge of her bed, her slim bare feet. Then their gazes caught and held again and, because of the long moment during which neither of them were able to break it, it was unspoken but obvious that a physical awareness of each other had come into play between them.

Fleur swallowed visibly and her fingers tightened on the towel as she wondered how to get across to Bryn Wallis that she had no intention of responding to this physical tension that had sprung up even though she couldn't deny it. But he was the one who broke the unseen form of electricity that was flowing between them. A frown grew in his eyes then he looked down at the coffee glass in his hands, and carefully put it down on her bedside table. And he strolled over to the only chair and sank down into it.

'The thing is,' he said, picking up his own glass and gazing at it reflectively, 'one of the problems I have is that you remind me of someone I don't particularly want to be reminded of. But…'

He paused and looked up at last. 'The far greater part of it is—you're too good to be true, Fleur. The most human thing I've seen you do is pour food and drink all over me. It's,' his lips twisted ruefully, 'unnerving to witness such a gorgeous twenty-three-year-old girl who is also so reserved and contained and buttoned up and—solitary.'

He looked around and continued, 'There's nothing here, no photos, mementoes, nothing—apart from some books. By the way, I have quite a library in my bungalow. Please feel free to help yourself.'

Fleur shook her head as if to clear it. 'Am I buttoned up with Tom?' she protested after a moment.

'No. But that's different—kids are easier to relate to.'

She was silent for a long time, then she said composedly, 'OK, I'm trying out a new kind of life. I woke up one day and discovered I was going down a road I didn't like, so,' she shrugged, 'I opted out. Would I be right in thinking you yourself might have opted out, Bryn?'

He smiled faintly. '*Touché*. On the other hand, has that steel-trap mind of yours perceived a difference between us? For example, I may have opted out of the rat race but I haven't cut myself off from people.'

Fleur raised her eyebrows. 'I had noticed that—I'm not blind,' she said wryly. 'A mind like a steel trap, though? Isn't that a bit of an exaggeration?'

'No,' he replied flatly. 'Otherwise I'd have broken you down a lot sooner, Ms Millar. Three and a half weeks of putting up with me at my worst, with such composure, definitely denotes a steely mind.'

Fleur's lips parted and her eyes widened.

'Which is not to say,' he mused, 'that I did actually break you down, not in the way I anticipated anyway. *No one*,' he emphasized, 'has ever thrown a drink in my face let alone poured raspberries and cream all over me. In fact,' he looked briefly gloomy, 'the honours go to you, Fleur, which is a little demoralizing, to be honest.'

Fleur struggled through several emotions then started to smile reluctantly.

'That's better,' he murmured and sipped his coffee.

'It's not really,' she denied. 'I only found it amusing that you've managed to escape that fate for so long, to be honest. Otherwise, you've admitted to being highly manipulative if nothing else.' She wrinkled her brow. 'What I don't understand is why you care one way or the other?'

He took another sip and said at length, 'In another life I was a journalist. Old habits, such as digging out the truth of things, die hard, I guess. So, going to tell me why you've decided there should be no more men in your life, Fleur?'

Fortunately Fleur had put her coffee glass down on the bedside table, otherwise the sheer accuracy of this observation might have seen her spill it. Even so, her restless movement didn't escape him.

'You don't need to be a genius to see that,' he said. 'Julene is of the opinion you got your heart broken and Eric thinks it might have happened a couple of times. Mind you, while they needed a couple of weeks to work it out, I did spot it straight away,' he said modestly.

Fleur sat up straighter and said in a strangled voice, 'You...you've all discussed it? Behind my back!'

He shrugged. 'Human nature.'

'No...I... Darn it, it's unforgivable...and *you*...' She could only glare at him.

He shrugged again. '*You* think that because of how much you *have* cut yourself off from the rest of the world. But nothing on earth would have stopped Julene having a good gossip about you, me included.'

'You didn't have to participate, though,' she said through her teeth.

He smiled crookedly. 'I didn't contribute that much. In fact it came up when Eric told me I was being extremely unkind to you.'

'What a pity you don't take more notice of Eric,' she shot back.

Bryn lay back in his chair. 'I do. Well, sometimes. Eric and I go way back and, on the whole, I've found his advice to be wise—I just wasn't in the mood to take it this time.'

Fleur stared at him incredulously, trying to sort through it all, then she closed her eyes and shook her head. 'It's like being in a madhouse,' she said.

'On the other hand, we just might be able to help.'

Her lashes lifted and a sudden thought came to her. 'Who do I remind you of? What part does that play in it all?' she asked slowly.

He finished his coffee and stood up. 'Oh, that was only fleeting and not really important. What is important, Fleur,' he paused and looked at her with a mixture of sympathy and seriousness—with absolutely *no* hint of that electric tension that had flowed between them before—and went on, 'is that you can talk to us. You really don't have to soldier on alone. But that's enough for one night—I'll leave you to finish your coffee in peace. Goodnight!'

Fleur listened to him walking down the veranda steps, then there was silence as the beach swallowed up his footsteps. She blinked several times, lay flat then sat up, shaking her head, and reached for her coffee with her mind in turmoil. How had she not realized that she came across as so obviously isolated and damaged? To the extent that people would gossip about it behind her back? Apart from Bryn's hostility to cope with, she'd thought she'd appeared tranquil and even enjoying her sojourn at Clam Cove—apart from him, she had been, damn it!

So was it another frustrating example of give a girl a pretty face and figure—and you only acquired those because of your genes—and, without a constant supply of men dancing attendance, people immediately assumed there was some trauma?

Well, there was, she thought ruefully, but whose business was it but her own?

She drained her glass and stood up to pace around her bungalow for a while. On the other hand, could she have landed amongst a bunch of fruit loops? And why did she have this conviction, despite Bryn's disclaimer about her reminding him of someone not being important, it was much more of a key to things than he'd been prepared to admit?

She stopped abruptly in the middle of the cabin as her conversation with Julene just that morning came back to her. What was it Julene had said—'You could have knocked us over with a feather when he produced you…' Yes, her exact words. Did this mean Julene and Eric knew who she reminded Bryn of? And to produce such a hostile reaction in him from the first moment they met—it had to be another woman in his life, she reasoned, a woman who had left her mark most unhappily on him...

Right on cue Tom's little face floated into her mind. Tom, whose mother was never mentioned, which in itself meant there had to be trauma, for whatever reason, associated with her memory. Was that what she'd walked into? Reminding a man of the mother of his child when he'd much prefer to forget her?

She came to life and turned off the oil lamp, shrugged out of her robe and slipped into bed as exhaustion suddenly hit her. Then she remembered what he'd said about being a journalist in a former life.

She sat up and pondered this. It explained the laptop Tom had told her about in his bungalow. It probably explained the light on in his bungalow at all hours. So did he still practise journalism? If so, why did he never mention it?

And before she fell asleep another dilemma raised its head with her. Her physical reaction to Bryn Wallis, and his to her, unless it had been her imagination...

Julene was up and about and apparently restored to normal when Fleur surfaced a little later than usual the next morning.

'Some night,' she said chattily as she sat down with a cup of coffee while Fleur ate her breakfast. 'I have to tell you Eric was most impressed.'

Fleur opened her mouth to ask what with, but decided to save her breath.

'He can't remember anyone giving Bryn as good as they got quite like that before,' Julene went on. 'Of course, I knew you had to crack eventually, he was being totally unreasonable and impossible but—raspberries and cream! Way to go, kid.'

Fleur smiled feebly.

'You're not feeling guilty?' Julene enquired with a frown. 'You see, it'll clear the air tremendously—by the way, all your clothes washed up on the beach. I reckon the shoes are ruined but a bit of bleach will get the stains out of his shirt; not so sure about your dress, though. If you don't mind me saying so, it wasn't the most attractive dress, so that could be a good thing—What's the matter?'

Fleur had stopped eating abruptly. Now she put her hands to her head and started to laugh helplessly. Finally she looked up at Julene with streaming eyes. 'Does this place ever strike you as a madhouse?' she asked.

'Well, now,' Julene started to laugh too, 'can't say things are ever boring around Bryn!'

Fleur sobered. 'I gather you're all worried about me? There's no need. OK, yes, I'm not into men at the moment—'

'They can be bastards,' Julene broke in sympathetically.

Fleur smiled mechanically then frowned. 'Can I ask you something?'

'Fire away, honey!'

'Surely it's better, after you've—' she shrugged '—got your fingers burnt, in a manner of speaking, to…retire for a bit? That's, well, one thing I'm doing, trying to build another life, I guess.'

'What was your previous life?' Julene asked curiously.

'Two years studying computer science and statistics after school then receiving an offer from a modelling agency I couldn't refuse—or so I thought at the time.

But it all palled, so,' she spread her hands palms outward, 'I decided to get my feet back on the ground.'

Julene reached for the percolator and poured herself another cup of coffee. She stirred sugar into it. 'You still need friends, hon,' she said thoughtfully. 'And what about your family?'

Fleur made a curiously helpless little gesture and said wryly, 'My parents are overseas travelling the world and I do keep in touch with them regularly via e-mail. The same with friends.'

Julene shrugged. 'I'd still feel happier if you got some letters or phone calls.'

Fleur bit her lip and for a moment was tempted to tell Julene why it made her extremely happy to receive no mail, no phone calls and especially no flowers at Clam Cove. But she stifled the urge—it was like living in a fishbowl here anyway.

So she changed the subject. 'Julene, who do I remind Bryn of?'

A flicker of indecision passed through Julene's eyes then she shrugged. 'Tom's mother, but that's something you should ask Bryn about.'

Fleur started to say something then changed her mind. 'Where is he? The place seems to be very quiet.' She looked around.

'He took Tom across to the mainland for a check-up.'

'Any spots?'

'Nope.' Julene stood up. 'He was as bright as a button this morning. Might have been a false alarm but he wanted to be sure. Oh, well, guess I'll finish clearing up the mess—by the way, the boss has decreed that we are closed tonight even though it's not a Monday.'

Monday was the one day of the week the restaurant didn't open.

'Glory be,' Fleur said with feeling. 'I'll give you a hand with the mess.' Her lips curved into a rueful smile. 'Since I caused a lot of it.'

Bryn didn't arrive home until late afternoon—minus Tom.

He came into Fleur's office just as she was preparing to knock off for the day and was massaging the back of her neck. She didn't hear him come back, didn't know he was in the office behind her until he said, 'Tired?'

She dropped her hand and turned to face him slowly. 'A little. How...how is Tom?'

Bryn looked her over thoroughly before replying. If anyone looked tired, he did, she thought in the pause, in his moleskins, check shirt and deck shoes. There seemed to be shadows beneath his eyes and more lines beside his mouth than she remembered, and she flinched inwardly because she didn't want to notice things like that about this man but didn't seem able to help herself.

'Tom appears to be fine,' he said at last. 'But friends of mine are holidaying on the mainland. They have a couple of kids round about his age and he knows them well, so I left him with them for a couple of days. They've both had chickenpox and their mum knows what to look out for in Tom.'

'Oh. Well, I guess he'll enjoy some company of his own age.'

Bryn smiled twistedly. 'So he gave me to understand. Like a drink?'

Fleur blinked. 'I...'

'Eric is setting up a barbecue on the beach and Julene is going to cook. We'll have the pleasure of Clam Cove to ourselves this evening.'

'That sounds…that sounds wonderful,' Fleur heard herself say with more enthusiasm than she could explain.

And after a moment Bryn Wallis smiled down at her more genuinely than he ever had before, causing her to catch her breath—and pray he hadn't noticed.

It was a wonderful evening. They swam, while the water was smooth, silky and coloured oyster with touches of fire from the setting sun. Eric built a fire and Julene grilled fillets of fish, heated crusty bread in the coals and provided a delicious risotto as well as a fresh salad to go with the fish, plus her homemade tartar sauce. They opened a couple of bottles of wine and sat in deckchairs on the beach—more relaxed than Fleur would have thought possible only a day ago.

Bryn built up the fire after they'd eaten and the swift darkness of the tropics fell. Then, in a rather orchestrated way, Fleur felt, Julene and Eric yawned simultaneously, claimed they needed an early night in the same breath, and departed for bed.

She was still looking surprised when Bryn started to laugh softly.

'What was that all about?' she asked.

'I have to agree they're lousy actors,' he said, still grinning.

'But why?' She looked even more puzzled.

'Fleur, your steely mind must be taking a break—I should have thought it was obvious.'

'Not to me. I feel as if I've suddenly acquired body odour.' She shrugged whimsically.

'Not at all. I'd say that Julene and Eric, with a consummate lack of subtlety, have decided to throw us together.'

Fleur's lips parted incredulously. 'But...I don't understand... Why?'

'They've obviously come to the conclusion we'd be good for each other.'

'Only last night,' she said, 'and for the past three and a half weeks it's been—' She stopped and gestured helplessly.

'The other side of a certain coin?' he broke in to say. 'Perhaps.'

In the silence that followed his statement, Fleur wished with all her heart that she could feign misunderstanding or deny it. She moved restlessly in her deckchair and shuffled her bare feet in the sand. It was another beautiful night with the Southern Cross hanging above their heads, and the fire was casting leaping shadows on the beach.

'You and I,' he said quietly at last, 'may have a better understanding of things, though.'

'Such as?'

'Such as why we don't wish to pursue the other side of the coin—I'm talking about the attraction that lies just beneath the surface.'

She released a deep breath and glanced at him through her lashes.

He had on the same football shirt and khaki shorts of the night before and he was lying back in his chair with his legs sprawled out, looking up at the stars.

He was, it would appear, relaxed and in a contemplative frame of mind, as if he was talking about something quite abstract and he was not, at that moment, prey to any physical attraction to her. Whereas just looking at his big frame sprawled in the chair as he gazed up at the stars brought a strange clenching to the stomach for her, for example.

'Go on,' she said, when she could keep her voice cool and calm.

He glinted a quizzical hazel glance at her and resumed his study of the heavens. 'Well, the reason you may not want to pursue it is because you, for whatever reason, have given up men.'

'And you?' she queried.

'Ah. It couldn't be said that I've given up women.'

'I had noticed that.'

He smiled. 'On the other hand, I have given up Stella.'

Fleur blinked. 'Why?'

'The same reason that would make it unforgivable for me to take up with you, Fleur. I'm perfectly happy to continue my bachelor existence. I don't say this with any pride but I'm a hard man to pin down—'

'I'd say there's a lot of pride in that statement, Bryn,' she interjected sharply. 'How did you fail to make Stella aware of this before you took up with her—or didn't you even try?' She looked across at him sardonically. But something in his expression arrested her. Something in the way he fleetingly lowered his eyelids made her wonder whether he was actually hiding cool amusement—and she'd walked into a trap of his devising.

'Bryn,' she said slowly, 'I'm not really interested in what reasons you may have for not wanting to take up with me—I'm just glad you have them.'

He sat up at last, to clasp his hands between his knees and subject her to a penetrating gaze that was also quite enigmatic. 'So we understand each other quite well?' he said at length.

'We do.'

'Hmm…'

A smile trembled on Fleur's lips but she forced it to disappear at the same time as she thought, Got you there, Bryn Wallis! Perhaps he read her thoughts, though, because the glance he then bestowed upon her was loaded with irony. 'So be it,' he murmured. 'By the way, I've decided to close again tomorrow night. Could you see your way clear to taking a day off, Miss Millar?'

Fleur frowned. 'I—'

'It's just that Eric and Julene want to take their yacht for a spin and there's a beach on the mainland with this marvellous waterfall and pool. It's a great spot for a picnic.'

She thought for a bit. 'And you don't think Eric and Julene will come up with another novel way to "throw us together"?' she queried.

He grinned. 'What do they say—forewarned is forearmed? I was also thinking of getting my friends and Tom to join us. They've got a four-wheel-drive, so they can get to this beach by road—track really. I would imagine all that should be sufficient to dampen any suspicious ardour we might feel for each other, don't you?'

'Bryn,' she responded swiftly and through her teeth, 'don't make me mad enough to want to throw another drink over you with that kind of clever satire!'

He blinked, looked at her fingers clenched around her wineglass and said gravely, 'Sorry. My ego just took another little dent, you might say.'

'You mean it's all right for *you* to tell me you don't

want to pursue me but it's a bit different for *me* to tell you I'm happy about it?' she responded tartly.

'I told you you had a mind like steel trap, Fleur, didn't I?' he marvelled, looking glum.

She stood up. 'Not really. But I do have some experience of men and their egos.'

His false expression of glumness faded, to be replaced by something alert and probing. Fleur bit her lip and wished she'd held her peace rather than making inflammatory remarks—she also knew enough about men to know that what she'd said would invite curiosity at the least. She discovered almost immediately that she was not wrong.

'How many have there been?' he queried. 'Men, I mean.'

'I've known dozens of men,' she replied.

'Allow me to rephrase.' He looked up at her as if to say, Two can play that kind of game. 'How many have you slept with?'

'It was not a profession with me, if that's what you're implying.' The firelight made her eyes look bluer—and very cynical.

Bryn swore beneath his breath and stood up to put his hands on her shoulders. 'Don't—'

'Don't you try to manhandle me again, Bryn Wallis,' she said through gritted teeth.

His fingers dug into her shoulders briefly then he shook his head savagely and released her. 'I was about to say, don't read things into everything I say before I've had a chance to say it, Fleur. But, even if it wasn't a profession,' he continued grimly, 'it's a road to destruction, Fleur. Hell, now look what you've done!' he finished bitterly.

She blinked several times and looked around in utter confusion. 'What?'

'I knew you'd get me all worried about you—that's why I didn't want you for the job!'

'I...I...but you hardly know me from a bar of soap,' she said confusedly.

'I know the type all too well,' he replied. 'Too gorgeous for your own good, Ms Millar, not to mention walking man-bait.'

Fleur's mouth fell open, then she snapped it shut. 'All right!' She was so angry it amazed her that her words came out crisp and crystal-clear. 'This was meant to be the path to redemption, Mr Wallis. But I can travel it on my own; I don't need help or anyone to worry about me—least of all you. In which case it might be an idea for you to go back to Stella, if that's what this is *really* about.' She put her hands on her hips to stare at him levelly, and saw him react sharply.

Then he took hold, folded his arms leisurely and summed her up comprehensively from head to toe. She'd put a thin white pullover on over her swimming costume, so her legs were bare, and his gaze lingered on them. Finally he drawled, 'What's that supposed to mean?'

'That you're finding it more difficult than you anticipated not to pursue me now Stella has palled,' she replied bluntly.

'Well, now.' He shrugged and rubbed his jaw reflectively, then he smiled. 'You could be right, Fleur. You could be right!'

She drew an outraged breath. 'And you still have the nerve to lecture me and sermonize about paths to destruction—I don't believe you, Bryn Wallis! Just don't think I...that I...will—' She couldn't go on and she did it again out of sheer frustration—emptied her wine-glass over him.

'Dear me,' he murmured in the moment before he reached for her, 'you're a regular little wild cat, Ms Millar. Maybe we just can't help ourselves?' he theorized at large, then shrugged again and pulled her into his arms.

Fleur gathered herself to resist him to the bitter end but all he did was look down at her for a long considering moment. Then he placed his lips gently against hers for a brief moment before letting her go. As a final insult, he patted her on the head, and strolled away down the beach towards his bungalow.

CHAPTER THREE

'FLEUR! Fleur!' Tom called excitedly the next morning, when they had landed on the beach after sailing across from the island to the mainland. 'I'm so glad you came! These are my friends, Lucy and Brad.'

Thank heavens for Tom, Fleur thought as she greeted Lucy and Brad gravely. At least his enthusiastic presence might relieve some of the deadly tension that had simmered between her and Bryn through breakfast, through the sail on the *Julene*, through anchoring the yacht offshore and coming into the beach by dinghy.

Not that Bryn had said anything to her that she could take exception to, the opposite if anything was true, but he'd been so unnaturally polite and courteous that even Julene had fallen silent beneath the weight of Bryn Wallis at his most contrary.

It was a blazingly hot day and all three children wore protective shirts over their costumes, kepi hats, and were liberally smeared with zinc cream. They chatted to her excitedly before running off to inspect a rock pool. Then she was being introduced to Moira and Ken Henderson, Lucy and Brad's parents, and Lyall Henderson, Ken's brother—introduced as only Bryn, in his present mood, could do it.

'This is Fleur, folks,' he said at large. 'The keeper of my books and the only person who has twice poured a drink over me—as well as a few other things. I just mention this in passing so you'll know what to expect should you tangle with her.'

Dead silence greeted this statement as everyone stared at Fleur bemusedly.

You bastard, Fleur thought, but managed to smile amusedly. 'I doubt if anyone could be as difficult or exasperating as you, Bryn, so I think they'll be quite safe from me,' she said ruefully and turned to the Henderson clan. 'How do you do? I'm so glad to see Tom looking better!'

It broke the ice. Everyone laughed and Ken Henderson said genially to Bryn, 'Met your match at last, boyo? Not before time if you ask me. I must say, though, Fleur, you've made a great hit with Tom. He hasn't stopped talking about you!'

A warm little feeling ran through Fleur as Moira seconded this sentiment, despite the fact that she could cheerfully have killed Tom's father. But, as the picnic got under way, Bryn got back to his other persona—funny and engaging, and she was not singled out for any more satirical treatment. All the same, as they climbed the cliff behind the beach to find the waterfall, she took care to stay well out of his way and, as they negotiated the narrow path, found herself paired with Lyall Henderson.

In his mid-twenties, she guessed, about her height, he had fair curly hair and an engaging smile. And they chatted on the way up so that she came to know he was a medical intern on holiday, that he lived in Brisbane, and had spent the first week of his break trying to catch up on some sleep.

It was a hot, steep climb beside a stream that bubbled down the hill over a bed of smooth round rocks. Cicadas shrilled in the bushes, green ants prowled along the branches of the melaleucas and banksias and a flock of white cockatoos screeched as they flew overhead, wheeled and came to rest in some huge gum trees.

'This is quite a climb,' Fleur said, wiping the sweat off her face.

'Not far now,' Lyall replied. 'And definitely worth it—you'll see!'

Five minutes later she did. The waterfall cascaded down into a natural basin of rock that provided a deep, clear pool.

'OK, kids,' Bryn said, 'last one in is a dummy!' And he dived straight into the water. The kids followed suit—they could all swim like fish—and one by one the adults followed after discarding shorts and shirts. Fleur was the last to go in, in her one-piece turquoise costume with a halter strap, and was amazed to find the water was cold but marvellously refreshing. You could also swim right under the waterfall and come up in a cave that was screened from the rest of the pool by a green curtain of water.

She did so, and as she surfaced Bryn came up beside her. They were the only two behind the waterfall as a lively game of Marco Polo was being played on the other side. And his faintly malicious smile told her that the truce had been temporary, but he chose to confirm it in words. 'Safest place to be in your company, Fleur! It would be hard to get wetter.'

She paddled to a ledge and pulled herself up to sit on it. 'Don't you think you might have got enough mileage out of that, Bryn?'

He swam to the ledge, rested his arms on it and propped his chin on his fist. 'If it had happened to you, you could think otherwise. As a matter of interest, do you not have any regrets at all about consistently dousing me in food and drink?'

'I always work on the premise that one should never regret something you do in genuine emotion. However,' she said gravely, 'your inability to keep things to yourself was not something I was aware of.'

'I am like that,' he agreed. 'Does that mean you'll restrain yourself in future?' He shot her a very hazel look.

She raised her eyebrows and sleeked back her hair. 'All depends. Being "typecast" and referred to as walking man-bait could make it a little difficult.'

'What about the gorgeous bit?'

Fleur had wound her hair up on top of her head and was holding it there. 'Gorgeous is as gorgeous does,' she said ruefully. 'There's got to be more to it than that, surely?'

I wonder, Bryn found himself thinking. Has she no idea how exquisite the curves of her breasts, hips and thighs are, how sleek and satiny and unblemished her skin is, how the lines of her body flow in perfect proportion, how classy that fastidious little nose is—and how grateful I am this water is as cold as it is?

Then he thought that perhaps she did know all those things, or that he'd been unable to hide his instinctive admiration, because she lowered her arms abruptly and the shape of her breasts changed although her nipples were still clearly outlined beneath the turquoise Lycra. She also slid into the pool a little clumsily and made to swim away from him.

'I'm surprised you're not a top model, Fleur,' he said.

She stopped swimming and turned back to him, treading water. 'I was,' she said slowly. 'Then I discovered that a lot of men are just like you, Bryn. Only interested in my body. Which is why, since it's obviously bugging you, I gave up men.'

This time she turned and swam round the waterfall.

He didn't follow immediately but stared after her with a frown in his eyes. And he posed a question to himself—what would he do in the normal course of events? Concentrate on her soul until the rest of it fell into place? A dry smile twisted his lips. But did he want to go down that road with this girl who brought back memories he'd rather forget, a girl who, he had the gut feeling, was just too gorgeous for her own good, and quite possibly his good?

Then he shrugged and reflected that he might not be able to help himself, if his behaviour to date was any example. Which had, not to put too fine a point on it, he thought moodily, alternated between being furiously exasperated with her, and a growing—he couldn't deny it—interest in that beautiful body. Dear me, Bryn Wallis, he told himself with considerable irony, could you be lumped into that 'men who only want one thing from women' category?

It was no consolation to think, at the same time, that Stella Sinclair might agree. Stella, he marvelled, a career woman through to her soul, whose path he had confidently thought would join his for a time then curve away to follow her ambitions.

Only to find that the offer of a promotion and a move to a much larger resort owned by the chain she worked for was not what Stella was seeking suddenly. Throwing her lot in with his, helping him to expand Clam Cove into an exclusive, wildly expensive, wilderness retreat was what Stella had had in mind—and he hadn't even seen it coming.

But how much of that blindness could be attributed

to Fleur Millar's entrance into his life? he mused grimly. He had certainly been less than sensitive to the turmoil building up in Stella after she had got the offer of promotion, which had just happened to coincide almost to the day with Fleur's arrival.

More to the point, he thought bitterly, why the hell hadn't he stuck to his guns and refused Fleur the job in the first place?

The picnic seemed never-ending to Fleur.

Not because it wasn't a pleasant, convivial one but because she felt restless and uneasy and was not quite sure why.

Yes, Bryn Wallis was part of it, although after their encounter behind the waterfall he'd been quite normal with her. But she might never be easy in his company again, she thought with a little inward shiver. Not after the way he'd mentally stripped her and not bothered to hide it. Not after she'd tingled from her scalp to her toes beneath that scrutiny and had a sudden vision of them both naked in that green-curtained cocoon behind the waterfall. Naked and with his hands on the paler, secret places of her body...

Then there was Lyall, not attempting hide that he would like to get to know her better and dancing attendance on her, although nicely.

But there was more to her sense of unease, she realized as the long hot day wore on and she played with the children, and Tom, when Lucy and Brad had curled up next to their mother, having temporarily exhausted themselves, came to curl up beside her.

'Tired, young man?' she said softly.

'No,' he denied stoutly then yawned mightily and looked the picture of guilt.

'Do you know what instinctive means, Tom?'

He screwed up his face. 'No.'

'It's something you do without thinking it out, as if this invisible thing inside you makes you do it. And all kids have this instinct *never* to admit they're tired.'

'Did you, Fleur?'

'I did! I guess it comes from a fear of being sent to bed when you really want to stay up.'

He considered then grinned at her. 'I hate being sent to bed! I never understand why I can't stay up as long the grown-ups do.'

'There you are, you see. You're just like all kids.'

'Have you got any kids, Fleur?'

She looked down at him. 'No. Why?'

'You seem to understand them pretty well,' Tom said sagely, then yawned again. 'You're also nice, Fleur, so I'll tell you a secret. I've had enough picnic, I'm tired of playing with Lucy and Brad—I was even starting to want to fight with Brad because he thinks he knows *everything*, and Lucy can be a real baby sometimes! And I feel funny, tired but not tired,' he gestured, a quaintly adult motion, 'and itchy with all this sand around. Beaches can get on your nerves sometimes, can't they?'

Two things struck Fleur simultaneously. The first was that some of her unease had come from being the only one in the party with no ties to anyone, but the thought grew suddenly—the only one with no family. Julene and Eric had each other. Tom and Bryn had each other, the Hendersons were obviously wrapped up in their children and Lyall was part of the family. She was the only loner, but it was worse...

A growing attachment to this particular child, who was such a character and starting to look so hot and bothered beside her, brought home to her how her expectations of life had been so different once... Having her own family, her own children by now had been her dearest wish once, and without that wish fulfilled she felt as if she were inhabited by a great void, and that was what a picnic at the beach amongst families and children had brought home to her to cause that restless unease.

She let out a long slow breath as if to expel some of the pain, and did the only thing she could—concentrate on the other thing that had struck her. 'Tom, let's look under your shirt. Maybe we can get the sand out. Just stand up for a moment.'

He did, she looked, and the evidence was incontrovertible. She glanced across at Bryn, to find him watching her, and gestured for him to come and look, because there was no doubt from the blisters across his tummy that his son had chickenpox.

Three nights later Fleur wandered into the main room of Bryn's bungalow. Tom was asleep, although for how long was another matter. She glanced at her watch. The restaurant would be in full swing now, and she had been invited to avail herself of her boss's library.

But she looked around first. Bryn's bungalow had four rooms—two bedrooms, a lounge, and off it, through a curtain of amber beads, a study. An *en suite* bathroom linked Tom's bedroom and Bryn's. It was all rather spartan, she decided, but not unattractive. Tom's bedroom had two single beds, hooks on the wall to hang clothes, a table and a chest of drawers. There was also a shelf for Tom's collection of wooden animals.

Bryn's room was equally as simply furnished although he had a double bed with a colourful Indian cotton throw.

The lounge opened on to the veranda, had two settees, one beautiful coffee table that Bryn had made himself, and plenty of bookcases. But it was the room through the beaded curtain that fascinated Fleur. During the days of nursing Tom she'd wondered about it but not had the nerve to investigate. Or was it that? she wondered. She certainly had no intention of prying, she just had this urge to look beyond the amber curtain. But it indicated an urge to know more about Bryn Wallis and that was what really worried her.

She shook herself mentally. It couldn't hurt just to have a look. She parted the beads but the room was in darkness, so she fumbled for a switch and an overhead light came on. It was very simple, small, and all it contained was a table and chair, a laptop computer and a printer on the table, and an old-fashioned roll-top desk. But one entire wall was covered with maps and charts. So what did he do on his computer at the dead of night?

And how come this room was a model of tidiness compared to what she'd first encountered of his paperwork to do with the restaurant?

She was still no further forward and she began to feel uncomfortable, although she was only standing in the doorway. But it was as if his spirit was in this small room, a very private part of Bryn Wallis, and it was with relief that she heard Tom stir and wake up. She dropped the beads and went thankfully back to him.

That same evening, but much later, Bryn came quietly into Tom's bedroom to find Fleur asleep next to Tom on the bed with a Harry Potter book spread face down across her chest.

They'd had a council of war on discovering Tom's chickenpox. The community nurse was stretched to the limit—there was a minor epidemic on the island—and, although Julene had been more than happy to nurse Tom, when Fleur had offered her services she had done so with typical Fleur logic.

Julene was indispensable to the running of the restaurant, she'd pointed out. So after two nights closed, unless he wanted to stay closed, it made much more sense for her, Fleur, to look after Tom for the three or so days that he would be feverish and miserable. The books could wait for a few days, she'd added with a lurking smile in his direction, whereas the fresh food-stuffs for the restaurant could not.

It had all mirrored his own thinking but had annoyed him that she should be so logical. He'd followed this line of thought and discovered that the rapport Fleur obviously shared with Tom also annoyed him in some subtle way he couldn't quite define other than to bring home to him yet again the ambivalence of his feelings towards Fleur Millar.

But as he looked down at her now a rush of tenderness came to him. She'd been wonderful with Tom. She'd bathed him frequently with some stuff that lessened the itchiness and kept him occupied with games and books, and they could frequently be heard laughing together. And just her cool, calm presence seemed to soothe him when he was feeling feverish and especially itchy.

And she looked so young, he thought, with her hair spread out over the pillow, her eyes closed. Younger, in her simple pink blouse and white shorts, even than the twenty-year-old he had originally thought her to be. But still, if he was an enigma to himself on the subject of Fleur Millar, he thought drily, she was as much of an enigma herself…

Then Tom moved and murmured in his sleep, and she sat up groggily. But Tom settled and she looked up, aware of Bryn's presence suddenly, and stiffened.

'Come,' he said very quietly. 'You deserve a good night's sleep.'

'What about you?' she objected although sleepily. 'You've been working all day.'

He was still in his pirate outfit, although he'd discarded his bandanna, and had come straight from the restaurant. But he shrugged. 'I'm OK. And I'll sleep right in here with him.' He gestured to the other single bed. 'But I'll walk you home first.'

She sat up, rubbed her face then looked around for her sandals. But before she had got a chance to locate them he picked her up in his arms. 'Don't worry about shoes.'

Surprise, plus that wooziness of mind after waking up too early from a deep sleep, held her silent. Then other things held her silent. The ease with which he carried her down the steps of his house and across the beach. The warmth of his body against hers, the width of his shoulders, the pure man aroma of him with just a dash of something exotic and spicy like cumin or coriander, from his cooking, no doubt. The way her cheek lay against his chest and the way she could feel the beat of his heart beneath his shirt like a steady lifeline…

He didn't look down at her until he stood her on her feet on her own veranda. Then she noticed that he was breathing a little raggedly. So was she but it was hard to say if it was the exertion for him or a combination of it and all the sensations she had felt. All the same, it produced a strange reaction in her, a suddenly tender feeling towards Bryn Wallis.

And it must have been that that prompted her to say softly, 'I think Tom will be better tomorrow. Not a hundred per cent, but the spots are starting to fade.'

He took her hand with a faint sigh. 'I don't know how to thank you for all you've done for him. I'm sorry I was a bit...ungracious about it all.'

She turned her face up to him with a look of surprise in her eyes. 'Were you?'

'Didn't you notice?'

'I...' She grimaced 'To be honest, there didn't seem to be anything new in your manner.'

'So I'm ungracious most of the time?'

She smiled but didn't agree or disagree.

He looked down at her hand in his and suddenly raised his eyebrows. 'You don't bite your nails any more.'

Her hand moved in his then she took it away. 'No. It was something I—well, being up here seems to have made me not want to do it any more. Bryn, if you're worried about Tom getting too wrapped up in me, don't. You're still the most important thing in his life.'

He hesitated, as if about to pursue the nail-biting issue, but to her relief said instead, 'What about you? You seem to have got really fond of him and you seem to be a natural with kids.'

Fleur flinched inwardly. But she said lightly enough, 'Always thought I'd like six but that could be a reaction to being an only child. Goodnight, Bryn. Thanks.' She turned to go in.

'Fleur,' he said then stopped frustratedly. 'Good-night.'

The next morning Lyall Henderson turned up at Clam Cove and asked Fleur to have lunch with him at the resort.

She was on the point of refusing; she and Tom, who was much better, as she'd predicted, were doing a jig-saw puzzle but Bryn, who was in the house and privy to it all, had other ideas.

'What an excellent idea, Lyall, old man! She defi-nitely needs a break. Off you go and put some glad rags on, Miss Millar, and I will finish the puzzle with Tom. I'll shout you a beer in the meantime, Lyall,' he added.

Annoyance at being treated like this glinted in Fleur's eyes briefly, then she shrugged and did as she was bid. Twenty minutes later she returned to Bryn's bungalow wearing a long filmy cyclamen-pink skirt, matching sandals and a silky white halter-neck top.

If Lyall looked slightly stunned at this gorgeous, ex-tremely man-bait outfit and Tom whistled spontane-ously, her boss reacted differently. He drawled, 'That should really set the cat amongst the pigeons.' And raised his beer glass at her in a mocking salute.

Fleur simmered inwardly, although she knew she'd deliberately provoked this reaction; she just wasn't sure why she'd set out to do it. It was the one exotic outfit she'd brought to Clam Cove, and perhaps she'd donned it because Bryn had told her to get out her glad rags? Or to show him that she didn't need him to direct her social life? Or perhaps she'd put it on as a warning to him, she theorized. 'I am what I am so stay away, you're right about me' kind of statement.

Unfortunately, in her annoyance, she'd failed to take into account the effect it would have on Lyall, and she should have. Because it had been clear at the picnic that he would like to get to know her better, although she honestly hadn't expected him to show up out of the blue.

Damn, she thought, I've fallen into a trap of my own making. I allowed myself to be needled by Bryn into this. Oh, well, I'll just have to cope as best I can...

So she said airily to her boss, 'See you later.' And patted Tom on the top of his head. 'Stay cool, dude,' she murmured to him.

He grinned impishly up at her—this was a ritual between them—and replied, 'Don't do anything I wouldn't, Fleur!'

Lyall had hired a 'moke', an open-sided vehicle that you could pick up from the jetty, and they drove to the resort with the wind rushing through their hair. She asked him if he was still sleeping a lot of the time and he laughed and said that he'd got over that—and anyway, Lucy and Brad made sleeping in difficult.

He also confided that the reason he'd come on holiday with his brother, his sister-in-law and his niece and nephew was that he and Ken had jointly inherited the holiday cottage they were all staying at; he and Ken were fishing partners from way back to their juvenile days and they'd made this annual pilgrimage for as long as he could remember.

'So nothing has changed despite Ken acquiring a wife and two children?' she asked with a glinting little smile.

Lyall looked rueful. 'Moira has made some changes,' he conceded. 'We no longer fish day and night and there are strict rules about shaving daily. There is also an embargo on "talking fish" at certain times of the day.'

'Poor Moira,' Fleur said with some feeling.

Lyall laughed, and they arrived at the resort.

It turned out to be a pleasant meal they shared on a terrace overlooking the sea, shaded by a white canvas umbrella.

And, perhaps inevitably, the conversation turned to Bryn. Lyall brought the subject up by asking Fleur how she'd met him and come to work for him.

She told him.

'I gather,' he said slowly, 'it hasn't been an easy relationship at times?'

Fleur raised her eyebrows. 'You gather right. Which came as a bit of a surprise because,' she paused, 'well, there's no denying he can be most charismatic when he wants to be. How,' she hesitated, 'well do you know him?'

'Not that well at all. He and Ken have been friends since their university days, when I was still at school.' He grimaced. 'But one knows *of* him, of course.'

Fleur would have loved to ignore this opening to find out a bit more about Bryn Wallis but found she didn't have the moral fibre or whatever was required not to say, 'I don't know anything about him other than that he was journalist in his previous life.'

'More accurately a war correspondent,' Lyall supplied, 'with more nerve than most. They said he had the reactions, instincts and coordination of jungle cat, which is how he survived at it for so long. But then he…just packed it in and came up here.'

Fleur stared at Lyall wide-eyed for a moment.

'Of course, running a restaurant is not a complete departure for him. The Wallis family owns and runs a chain of prestige hotels…' Lyall named a couple '…all built up by his father and grandfather from one small inner-city café.'

This time Fleur blinked dazedly because one of the hotels Lyall had named was where she'd had her interview with Bryn. 'Not that he and his father see eye to eye much, according to Ken,' Lyall continued. 'You know, the age-old problem of fathers wanting their sons to follow in their footsteps but when Bryn gets this alternative-lifestyle syndrome out of his system, who knows?'

'I'm not so sure,' she said with a faint tinge of humour. 'He may cook like an angel but the only reason I'm here is to help him sort out the chaos he got himself into on the business side of the restaurant!'

Lyall laughed.

'So he comes from a wealthy background?' Fleur asked with a frown.

'Very wealthy. He and his sister, Alana, were consistently featured in the beautiful-people-born-with-a-silver-spoon set. Funny thing, though, she dropped out too and hasn't been sighted for years.'

'What about…Tom's mother?' Fleur asked because she couldn't help herself.

Lyall shrugged. 'It's always been a big mystery but Bryn has never lacked for women in his life. But hey! Enough of him! We're leaving in a couple of days, but, by my calculations, you should be back in Brisbane in a couple of months. May I keep in touch in the meantime?'

'I…' Fleur hesitated because he looked so earnest and he was nice.

Then he proved he was intuitive too. 'Just friends unless you would like it to be more?'

She smiled. 'That's easy to say, Lyall, but...'

'I hereby guarantee to absolve you of all responsibility for my feelings in the matter. And if you change your mind before you get back to Brisbane, all you have to do is not answer my letters.'

She looked down at the delicious prawn cutlets she was eating then up into his blue eyes and simply smiled faintly.

He sat back, apparently satisfied, and they finished their lunch in pleasant harmony.

But as they stood up to go a note of disharmony introduced itself. Stella Sinclair got up from a nearby table; Fleur hadn't noticed her, and she came over to them.

'Hi, Fleur,' she said casually enough.

'Oh—hello, Stella! Uh, this is Lyall Henderson. He's on holiday on the mainland.'

'How do you do?' Lyall said politely.

But Stella only studied him for a long moment then looked back to Fleur, deliberately taking in the lovely outfit Fleur wore. 'Wasn't stealing Bryn enough for you, Fleur?' she asked arctically. 'I wouldn't have thought you needed to import lovers from the mainland just yet, not with Bryn in tow, anyway, unless—that's the kind of woman you are!' And she turned on her heel to stalk away.

'Don't,' Lyall said and took Fleur's hand in his.

'What?' she asked shakenly.

'React at all. Let's just sweep out of here with our heads held high! Bryn,' he said drily, 'has been discarding women all his life, from what I've heard.'

Fleur started to walk. 'So you don't think I may have stolen him from her?'

'No. Which is not to say I don't think you'd be much safer with me than Bryn Wallis.'

'Has young Lochinvar ridden back to the mainland?'

Fleur stared at Bryn, who was the first person she'd happened to encounter after Lyall had dropped her off at Clam Cove. 'He's taken the ferry back to the mainland if that's what you mean,' she said coldly. She hadn't changed yet but come into her office to check if there were any faxes or e-mails before she made her way to her cabin. 'How's Tom?'

'Asleep at the moment. Good lunch?' he enquired, lounging against the doorpost. His hazel gaze skimmed her lovely outfit, her wayward, windblown hair, and came to rest on her mouth, almost as if he was speculating on whether she had been kissed or not.

In fact he stared at her mouth for so long, Fleur found herself licking her lips and remembering the feel of his lips on hers, although so brief, a few nights ago.

He looked up into her eyes at last, and she couldn't look away. Nor could she help the faint tinge of colour that came to her cheeks, and then she saw a little glint of triumph in his greeny-gold eyes, and knew he'd not only deliberately planned to jog her memory but had been able to read from her reaction that he had. Damn him, she thought and took a steadying breath.

'A great lunch,' she responded evenly, 'but I would appreciate it if you could disabuse your former mistress of the idea that I stole you from her.'

'Oh, dear,' he said plaintively. 'I gather Stella made a scene?'

'What I can't work out is why she would think that—unless you planted the seeds of it.'

'I did no such thing. Well,' he shrugged, 'you're a bit hard for anyone to ignore, Fleur—'

'Don't start that,' she broke in. 'I have no idea why you broke up with Stella, it's none of my business anyway, but one thing I do know—it had nothing to do with me!'

'She wanted to turn this place into a wildly expensive wilderness retreat where we socked the guests for close to a thousand dollars a day for the opportunity to get back to nature.'

Fleur stared at him with her lips parted, her eyes wide. 'You mean…here?'

'Here. Clam Cove. Where we are, at this minute, standing.'

Fleur closed her mouth with something of a snap then looked confused. 'But…why?'

He smiled faintly. 'She didn't begin to understand me for one thing.'

'She wouldn't be alone in that,' Fleur commented drily.

'You, on the other hand, looked quite shocked at the thought of the kind of desecration she had in mind for Clam Cove. I mean, the restaurant is bad enough, I sometimes think. And perhaps you also agree with me that *charging* people an arm and a leg to get back to nature is contrary to the true spirit of the thing anyway?'

Fleur blinked several times then spread her hands. 'Look, there's no point debating what you and I may or may *not* agree upon. The thing is, she thinks it happened because of me!'

He was silent.

'Was this only a business partnership she had in mind?' Fleur asked at length.

'No.'

'Would…she have been happy just to…live here with you, live *your* kind of life, I mean?'

Bryn grimaced. 'It's my considered opinion Stella will always be a career woman, although at the moment she's not seeing that too clearly.'

Fleur pulled out her chair and sank down into it. Bryn did not change his lounging position against the door frame, although he raised a hand to fiddle with the shark tooth hanging around his neck. He wore board shorts as usual and a faded yellow T-shirt.

'It would have happened, Fleur, whether you were here or not, and Stella will realize that in the course of time. But the blame does lie with me—I should have seen it coming. I didn't. I thought we were two of a kind in the wanting no commitment department,' he said and looked over her head at a spot on the wall. Then he added, 'I still think living my kind of life would have seen her tearing her hair out eventually.'

'Do you think you will always want to live this kind of life, Bryn?' Fleur heard herself say suddenly.

It was a long moment before he withdrew his gaze from the spot on the wall and looked at her. 'Who knows? How did you get on with Lyall?'

Fleur reacted to this blatant change of subject by standing up abruptly. 'Fine,' she said evenly. 'I think I'll go and change.'

But he straightened up so he was barring the doorway. 'I can vouch for him being a nice young man.'

'I would agree, although I didn't think you two knew each other that well.'

Their gazes locked then he shrugged. 'I don't. But

I'm a good judge of character and he comes from a nice family. I also think it's better for you to confine yourself to younger men. You might not get... exploited so frequently.'

Fleur closed her eyes then lifted her lashes to look at him steadily. 'Bryn, just move so I can get out of here, will you? I'm really not interested in your thoughts on the subject—and it's a pity you weren't a better judge of what was happening to Stella here and now, rather than your long-term judgements of her character.'

'I hate to be trite but it always amazes me how women stick together—even after she intimated you were a nymphomaniac! Be my guest,' he added, and stood aside with a flourish.

But Fleur was suddenly rooted to the spot. 'How did you know what she said?' she gasped.

'One of the resort waitresses is a great friend of Julene's. She just happened to be in earshot and she also just happened to be coming off her shift so she rang to impart this delicious tidbit of gossip—who wouldn't have? Especially on an island where we all know each other.'

Fleur ground her teeth. 'You mean a fishbowl! If only I'd known,' she marvelled.

He reached out a hand and placed the tip of his finger on the point of her chin for a moment. 'It's got to be better than working in an office, in a high-rise, in a city, surely?' There was quizzical amusement in his hazel eyes. 'It's got to be better *living* rather than just existing, for that matter.'

She started to say something scathing but it occurred to her suddenly that he had a point, although she wasn't sure why this feeling had crept over her from nowhere.

This feeling that she was making heavy weather of things for no good reason.

Then she noticed, through the open doorway, the pair of resident plovers with their black caps and yellow beaks, patrolling the lawn behind the restaurant. She often watched them through her office doorway, as well as the noisy throng of greenies, brilliant emerald and scarlet parrots that swooped in and out of the native bush beyond the lawn in search of succulent berries. And she often paused from her computer work and turned her chair to stare at the riotous tangle of purple bougainvillaea and yellow allamanda that covered an outbuilding, and the blue sky above.

What she thought at times like those, when she could also smell the tang of salty air on the breeze and hear the lap of the high tide on the beach, was how serene and beautiful Clam Cove was, and how much she enjoyed living there despite Bryn Wallis.

In fact, she realized, there were other times that gave her the same contentment. Times when she watched Bryn set out in the dinghy to check the lobster pots or fish from the beach. Times when she watched him contentedly working on a piece of wood in his studio which was nothing but a thatched roof on four poles with roll-down canvas walls to keep out the weather. And they gave her that sense of contentment because it seemed to epitomize the spirit of Clam Cove and what a haven of peace and creativity it would be in the months when the restaurant was closed.

She also, at those times, felt a stirring within to work with her hands and be productive in an earthy sense rather than be working on a computer. Also to be creative herself, and she found herself thinking of the wall hangings she and her mother had used to make, and felt a longing to incorporate the sea, the coral, the sky into glorious hangings…

'Fleur?'

She came back to the present and looked into Bryn's eyes. 'You could be right,' she said quietly. 'OK, no more drama. Would you like me to sit with Tom this evening?'

For a long moment there was something acute and probing in his eyes, then he smiled, that genuine smile that had a tendency to make her catch her breath, and replied, 'I'd really appreciate it.'

CHAPTER FOUR

For the next few days, Fleur soaked up the peace and contentment of Clam Cove. She did think of what Bryn had revealed about his affair with Stella, and concluded that, while he may not have been in the right, he was probably right in that Stella had failed to understand him.

And, as Tom recovered fully, things got back to normal. No, better than normal, she reflected. Because all the hostility seemed to have gone out of her relationship with Bryn. If he still thought of her as man-bait or exploitable by older men, he treated her quite differently. He even started to teach her how to fish from the beach, and hugged her good-naturedly when she caught her first fish—anyone would have thought she'd caught a pot of gold, so excited was she by one small whiting.

On another occasion, she came across him reading a newspaper which he then hurled away from him in obvious disgust.

This was not an infrequent event but she managed to say without revealing her amusement, 'Something bugging you, Bryn?'

'Yes!' He ground his teeth. 'Politicians making huge, meaningless promises to protect the environment when they would have not the slightest idea how to even go about it.'

'And you do?' She couldn't resist it.

His gaze sharpened on her. 'You think I don't?'

'I don't know. You do seem to have a lot of pent-up ire on a lot of subjects.'

'I happen to be very well read,' he said in a dignified way. Then his expression changed to one of rueful amusement. 'However, I am a firm believer in not believing everything you read—it's impossible anyway; you'd go mad because everyone contradicts everyone else!'

Fleur agreed that she'd suffered the same problem. 'I often think you have to go and see for yourself,' she added. 'But I'm sure you would know that better than most.'

His gaze narrowed on her. 'Would you be interested in doing that?'

She thought for a bit. 'Research and statistics have always appealed to me. Perhaps it's,' she glinted a laughing little look at him, 'why computers also appeal, as a way of reducing chaos to order.'

'As you have done with my business affairs?'

'Well, nearly.'

He opened his mouth as if to say more but Tom skipped up and they turned their attention to him.

And, by accident, she revealed a talent she had hitherto concealed. She came across Julene one afternoon, staring dismally at a pavlova she'd taken out of the oven.

'I hate making pavs,' Julene said intensely. 'Look at this, as flat as a pancake and Bryn's are sometimes no better. Why he insists on having them on the dessert menu is a mystery to me!'

'I…seem to have a bit of luck with them,' Fleur commented. 'Don't know why. I'm not in your or

Bryn's class otherwise when it comes to cooking, but pavs...' She shrugged.

Julene immediately reached for another apron and handed it to Fleur. 'Be a honey and have a go!' she begged.

So Fleur cooked a pavlova, cursing herself for ever mentioning it and quite sure her skill would desert her. It didn't. It was magnificent and she filled it with kiwi fruit, strawberries and cream. There was one small piece left over at the end of the evening when they were all sitting down having a cup of coffee, and Bryn ate it.

'Good-pavlova day,' he complimented Julene, and paused. 'Sensational-pavlova day!'

'I cannot tell a lie,' Julene said. 'I had an awful-pavlova day today and Fleur came to the rescue.'

Bryn switched his hazel gaze to Fleur with a definite tinge of surprise in it. 'You made this?'

'Er...yes. But it's about my only cooking forte,' she added hastily.

'How can you cook superb, melt-in-the-mouth pavlovas and nothing else?' he demanded.

'Well, perhaps it's because I like cooking desserts.' She shrugged.

'Fleur, would you like a rise in pay?'

She stared at him cautiously. 'What for?'

'Pavlovas, what else? And any other fabulous desserts you can come up with.'

'It would cut into my time with your books,' she pointed out.

'Blow the books. Look,' he said earnestly, 'that's what this place is all about. Excellence in what we do with our hands, not the books. Anyway,' he studied her keenly, 'I've got the feeling you could cope with the books with one hand tied behind your back.'

Fleur was silent for a time as she remembered her urge to be creative. Then she raised her eyebrows. 'OK. If it's OK with you, Julene?'

'Hon, I've just decided I'll never make another pavlova in my life!'

They all laughed.

That was how Fleur became the assistant dessert cook, and it wasn't long before she was producing not only magnificent pavlovas but also sticky date puddings, brandy puddings, light-as-air lemon meringues, sorbets, orange wedges in Cointreau and raspberry mousse.

It was as she was carefully separating orange segments one day that she looked up to find Bryn watching her thoughtfully. Nor did he stop watching her with that same thoughtful air until she said a little awkwardly, 'What have I done?'

'Do you realize how word of your puddings has spread?'

'Has it?'

'Yes. I had one couple from Melbourne tell me that was the reason they came to Hedge Island.'

'You're joking!'

'No. Friends of theirs who stayed here recommended the resort but added a rider that whatever they did they should not bypass the desserts at Clam Cove.'

'Oh! Didn't I tell you right at the beginning that I might bring in more guests for you?' she returned impishly.

'That too,' he murmured.

Fleur sobered. When she worked in the restaurant nowadays she was just her normal, natural self and she made no attempt to wear deliberately dowdy clothes. But she never responded to any overtures from male guests, although she couldn't say they didn't happen. Had he been observing them? she wondered now. Had it, despite her lack of response, added to his mistaken image of her as man-bait?

Then he smiled suddenly. 'It was a useful lesson in ego management.'

Fleur blinked.

'I was fully expecting to be told it was the lobster or my garlic prawns, my veal dishes or my magnificent roast pork.' He shrugged and looked downcast.

'I'm so sorry,' she said on a smothered laugh. 'I'm sure all those get talked about down south too!'

'And I know when I'm being humoured,' he returned, then came past her to casually rumple her hair. 'Keep at it, kid. You have a growing reputation to maintain.'

She stared after him as he walked away, with the sharp little knife she was using on the oranges poised. And it was some time before she got back to slicing segments as she grappled with the irony that things were so good between her and Bryn sometimes now, one would almost imagine the attraction between them that he hadn't denied should be allowed to...

Prosper, Fleur? she asked herself.

It was a question she found she couldn't answer. What she did know was that it was impossible not to like him more and more. And that it was becoming a concern to her to think that he viewed her as man-bait or a wild child, a girl to stay away from because of a misconception about her. Not only a concern but it also hurt...

And she couldn't deny it was less and less solely as

a friend that she thought about him when she couldn't monitor her thoughts…

She stared at the oranges she was working with, and wondered helplessly what was happening to her.

Things changed one balmy evening.

They had an unusually difficult dinner guest, a cigar-smoking man in his forties. He objected to not being allowed to smoke in the restaurant, he loudly condemned the wine list as unimaginative, he sent back his first course untasted because he didn't like the look of it—and his poor wife sat through it all with a frozen smile on her face.

Fleur was the receptionist for the evening and she, Julene and the waitress held their breath as Bryn's expression grew more and more murderous.

The *coup de grâce* came when a magnificent dish of Lobster Mornay was set before the guest, he tasted it—and sent it back too because the lobster was not fresh, in his opinion.

Fleur knew it was going to happen but not quite in the way she expected. Bryn descended leisurely from his cooking station with one hand behind his back and addressed the man quite genially…

'Mate,' he said, 'you may not realize this but I have been instructed in the art of giving people their come-uppance by an expert. You start off with a glass of wine.' He picked up the man's wine and studied it for a moment. 'Should be red wine for maximum effect but this will do.' And he poured it over the guest's head.

'Then,' he continued and revealed what he had in his other hand; a jug, 'you add some cream,' he poured the contents of the jug down the man's shirt front, 'and

you finish off with raspberries—excuse me, ma'am!'
He reached for the plate in front of the woman at the
next table, which just happened to be almost full of
raspberry mousse, and consigned it where the cream
had gone.

'Now, sir,' he said to his transfixed guest, 'you look
as foolish as you sound!' And he turned to Fleur to
add, 'I made a good pupil, didn't I?' He then stalked
out of the restaurant and disappeared.

An hour later Fleur found him standing on the beach,
staring out to sea.

She came up to him quietly, and when he said nothing simply stood beside him, until presently he roused
himself to ask, 'Am I to be charged with assault?'

'No.'

He turned his head to her. 'So what did happen?'

Fleur smiled faintly. 'Quite a bit of chaos until
Julene took command. The man's wife started to laugh
hysterically and to tell him that he deserved everything
he'd got.'

Bryn groaned.

'As you say. The man himself did mention, although
not very intelligibly, that the police should be called,
and the lady whose raspberry mousse you poured all
over him started to cry.'

Bryn dropped his head into his hands with another
groan.

'Cheer up,' Fleur advised. 'Don't forget that's the
other part of the lesson—never regret what's been done
when you're delivering come-uppances.'

He lifted his head to look at her ruefully. 'You must
have more intestinal fortitude than I do. Go on, what
happened then?'

'That's when Julene descended, and took over. I must say she was magnificent. Eric also appeared on the scene and she handed over the soggy guest to him to be taken away and cleaned up. You don't argue with Eric,' she said reminiscently.

'No,' Bryn agreed.

'Then she announced that no one would be charged for their dinner to compensate them for any distress they may have suffered during the incident, and she invited them back tomorrow night for a special evening she intended to plan.'

Bryn started to laugh. 'She did that? How very generous of Julene on my behalf.'

'It was good business—they all booked in for a repeat performance. She also vouched for the fact that the lobster had been caught this morning. In fact, everyone responded well and something like a party spirit developed as they were leaving.'

'What about the man's poor wife?'

'Ah. I don't know how Eric did it but he somehow conveyed to her husband that taking anything out on *her* would be unacceptable behaviour. He also personally drove them back to the resort.'

'And all's well that ends well,' Bryn murmured. 'So why do I feel like a bloody fool?'

Fleur started to laugh. 'It was one of the funniest things I've ever seen.'

'You think so?'

'I do—after I got over the shock of being your mentor, so to speak.' She was still smiling.

'I wasn't sure how you'd take that,' he said wryly.

For some reason this made Fleur start to laugh again and then he put his arms around her and they were laughing together.

'You are a character, you know,' she said unsteadily. 'I don't think I've ever met anyone quite like you!'

'The same goes for me,' he responded gravely. And lowered his head to kiss her.

Fleur could never afterwards claim immunity from a full and open response to this. The truth was, she felt closer to Bryn Wallis than she'd felt to anyone for a long time. The truth was, it was lovely to be held in his arms, to be warmed, to feel such a laughing kinship with a man, and it seemed like the most natural thing in the world to kiss him in return.

But if it started out in laughing kinship, it soon developed into something electrifying. The taste, the feel, the shape of him was so satisfying to Fleur she could only describe herself as revelling in being in his arms. All the sensations he aroused in her body as his hands travelled at will over her curves and slender lines felt unique to her, and as if anything she'd ever felt before were pale imitations of this stunning proximity, this intimate exploration of all her senses, by this man.

He kissed her throat and she shivered with pleasure. He slipped his fingers beneath the fine grey wool pullover she wore with a long black skirt and circled her breasts. She shivered again, this time with anticipation, and made a husky little sound in her throat as his hands moved away to circle her waist. She tossed her hair back and cupped the back of his head, offering him her mouth again. He obliged and she had to suffer the twin delight of being kissed deeply and feeling his hands roam intimately across her hips beneath the thin stuff of her skirt.

And all the time she was pressed against the hard length of him, and loving it as their bodies moved together, and she felt as if she was on fire from her head to her toes with the contact. On fire and gloriously aroused as well as gloriously aware of and pleasured by Bryn Wallis, of all men, whom she had often thought she hated. Then again, she thought as all this went through her mind like a surge of joy wrapped in a gold tissue of delight, she had always known he would be special in this way.

It was there in his lean, strong lines, there in his eyes, his hands, even there in all the contradictions of his quirky personality. It was there because you knew he was dangerously attractive and not necessarily in the conventional way, although he was that too. But he was also a man who'd taken danger in his stride, a man of many parts and talents, a man you could rely on in almost any situation…

Stop! she thought suddenly. Where was this leading? Remember, no more men…

Did he read her mind? she was to wonder later. Because he stopped right on cue. No, that wasn't right, she thought dazedly. He was letting her down slowly. His hands went from inflicting delight on her body, even celebrating it, to simply holding her gently. His lips left hers, then he kissed the top of head and withdrew his hands from her body altogether, to briefly gather her hair and smooth it. Then she was standing alone and he was about a foot away with his hands shoved into his pockets, looking out to sea again.

'What…what happened?' she asked unsteadily. 'I mean…*how* did it happen?' She stopped frustratedly.

He turned to her with one eyebrow raised. 'Because of a mutual hunger that's been growing between us from the moment we met?'

Fleur sat down suddenly on the beach with her legs

crossed and distractedly began to sift sand through her fingers.

'You can,' he said after a time, looking down at her bent head and working fingers, 'come up with all sorts of reasons for it not to be a good idea to feel this hunger. But I don't think you can—intelligently—deny its existence.'

'One of your "all sorts of reasons", no doubt, being that you don't want to commit to anyone,' she said drily.

'Do you?'

Fleur stopped sifting sand and stared out to sea. 'No. And least of all to you.'

'Could you say that in my arms, kissing me?' he queried with a touch of irony.

'Bryn,' she swallowed, 'you're doing it again. The last time we had this kind of conversation, you switched your stand on things from—'

'It's all right for me to lay down the law but not all right for you to agree?' he broke in to suggest ruefully. 'I'm only surprised you haven't credited me with a dog-in-the-manger stance on this.'

'Since you mention it,' she responded swiftly, 'it does sound rather apt.'

'So what are we going to do about the times when you just can't help yourself, Fleur?' It was said coolly and found its mark unerringly.

She flinched visibly but managed to regroup, or so she thought. 'It wasn't me alone! I mean...' She tapered off.

'Precisely. We each have our reasons but that's not going to help us when the going gets...hot again. So what I'm trying to say is not dog-in-the-manger stuff but that, rather than be deadlocked, we need to sort some things out.'

She stood up with a sigh and shook out her skirt. 'I've got a better idea. Why don't you just get someone else to sort out your impossibly tangled business affairs?'

'All right,' he drawled. 'If you want to fly the white feather, if you want to run away to bury yourself somewhere else, do it.'

'Why shouldn't I?' she flashed at him. 'Or would you rather see me end up like Stella, all bitter and twisted and—?' She broke off abruptly and bit her lip.

'Now that,' he said softly but lethally, 'is an admission I guess you're going to regret, Fleur.'

She closed her eyes and could have killed herself. So she took the next best option. She whirled away from him and fled up the beach to her bungalow.

There seemed to be only one remedy for an extremely restless night when Fleur gave up and got up the next morning before the sun rose—a swim. But because she didn't require any company—it was the last thing she wanted—she put on a pair of sand shoes, and shorts and a T-shirt over her costume, and set out for a little beach she'd found one day when she'd been exploring, on the other side of the headland from Clam Cove.

There was a path, of sorts, but also some rocks to climb over and some steep, tricky patches to negotiate. But the scenery was beautiful, with soaring hoop pines reaching up to a sky that was shot with streaks of pink and gold as the sun cleared the horizon like a ball of fire.

She paused at the top of the headland and looked out to sea before she began her descent. The water was like bright glass with the fiery splendour of the rising sun reflected on its surface. No suspicion of a breeze ruffled it, no swell contoured the surface, and a white yacht slid through it under power without its sails raised. A perfect day, she mused, unless you were hoping to sail.

Ten minutes later she was on the beach, a much smaller beach than Clam Cove but utterly private. So private, in fact, that when she'd stripped off her shoes, shorts and T-shirt she was suddenly tempted to strip off her costume as well. It was like a primitive urge to be at one with nature, at one with this beautiful morning—or perhaps even an urge to strip away all the mental turmoil and baggage she was struggling with at the moment, and cleanse herself ritually in the sea.

She hesitated then moved her towel and clothes as close to the line of water as possible without getting them wet. And she did remove her costume, laid her towel over it, and ran into the water with her arms wide, then raised them over her head and dived beneath the surface.

It was exquisite, she decided. It was cold but bracing and amazingly different from wearing a swimsuit. It felt marvellously free, perfectly natural and it somehow gave her the feeling she was purged of all her problems and in control of her destiny…

Which proved to be a false feeling, as it happened, because after swimming towards the far headland then turning to swim back she suddenly saw that she wasn't alone. Not only that but the dark copper hair of her fellow swimmer, even plastered to his head, was quite distinctive—it was Bryn.

She stopped swimming and trod water vigorously but he continued leisurely towards her. She opened her mouth to tell him to stop but got a mouthful of water instead and coughed, croaked and spluttered before she finally called, 'Go away, Bryn!'

He stopped a fair way off and trod water himself. 'Why?'

'Because I want to be alone! I didn't think anyone ever came here!'

'Well, I do, quite frequently.'

'So I gather,' she retorted bitterly. 'But how come I didn't see you when I came in?'

He looked back. 'I went round the point. There's a cave you can get into at the right tide and there are often lobster under the rocks. But my clothes are under that tree.' He raised an arm and pointed to the beach.

Fleur looked and noticed what she hadn't noticed before, a small pile beneath a flowering cottonwood with its boughs bent almost to the beach. 'Damn,' she muttered to herself as she trod water so vigorously as to create small waves around her. 'Uh…well, may I make a respectful request? I'd very much appreciate it if you'd go on your merry way and leave me to finish my swim in peace.'

He put his head to one side thoughtfully. 'There is one problem, Fleur.'

'*What?*' Her attempt to adopt a conciliatory manner deserted her.

'I am, not to put too fine a point on it, as naked as the day I was born. It's the kind of morning that just begs you to skinny-dip—me, anyway,' he said ruefully. 'So, in deference to your finer feelings, here's what I suggest. That you exit this delightful spot first.'

Fleur sank beneath the surface in sheer frustration. She came up, streaming water like a mermaid to her shoulders, and bit the bullet. 'I can't. But I can turn away and close my eyes while you get out.'

'Fleur!' His tone exhibited ingenious surprise. 'Don't tell me you're skinny-dipping as well?'

'I am. But before you attempt to dissect it or attribute all sorts of weird motives for it, may I say—it just seemed like a good idea at the time. I was wrong but I had no idea anyone was around.'

'I gathered that.'

'You... What do you mean?' she asked dangerously.

'I had just come round the point, and was obviously not visible against the rocks, when this—marvellous vision was afforded to me,' he explained. 'A beautiful girl shedding her clothes, after some hesitation and glancing around admittedly, then joyfully plunging into the water.' He paused. 'But what really intrigued me, Fleur, was that we were of the same mind.'

Fleur digested this and discovered that it took some of the sting out of her annoyance at being 'set up'.

'I...I...' she said slowly '...yes, I guess I felt the morning did just beg it. My state of mind seemed to beg it too,' she added honestly and a little sadly.

He swam up to her without her permission and looked into her eyes. 'John Donne wrote a line. ''Teach me to hear mermaids singing...'' That's what I thought of when I saw you earlier. Don't,' he paused, 'stop singing because of me.'

Her eyes widened.

'I also have a flask of hot coffee on the beach, only one cup but two fresh rolls, some butter and some jam.'

Her lips quivered. 'If that's an invitation to share your coffee and rolls, I don't think I can resist it.'

He smiled, and the little golden flecks in his hazel

eyes seemed to dance. 'You can go first, then. I will
confine my attentions out to sea.'

She grimaced. 'Then I turn my back while you come
out? Let's just do it quickly and together. See you at
the beach.' She struck out strongly.

As soon as she reached the beach, first, she picked
up her towel and wound it around her. Then she picked
up her shorts and shirt, and, without looking to see
where he was, disappeared behind a large boulder.
When she emerged, clothed and combing her fingers
through her hair, he was dressed and pouring the coffee.

'There you go, have the first cup,' he invited, but,
as their gazes caught then they both looked away, she
thought she detected something noncommittal in his
eyes, something that seemed to suggest a withdrawal.

She accepted the cup and thought for a moment.
'Thank you,' she said at last, 'and not only for the
coffee. But also for…making me feel like a mermaid
who could sing. Again. Perhaps.'

He grimaced. 'Was it so bad?'

She sank down on a log and cupped the coffee with
her hands. Then she inhaled the lovely aroma and
slowly drained the cup. She handed it back to him and
took the roll he offered her.

'I guess it started when I took up modelling. I was
twenty and—confused. I'd done this computer course
but my mother insisted that there was more to life than
that. My parents…' She shrugged suddenly. 'It doesn't
matter. I—'

'Yes, it does,' he broke in. 'I know it gets to a stage
when it's futile to blame your parents, but it does have
a bearing.'

She sent him a considering blue gaze. 'My mother

really wanted me to be an actress. To that end she insisted on putting me through drama classes, deportment classes, singing, dancing and elocution classes, you name it.' She waved a hand. 'My father maintained that I'd be far better off using my brains rather than my looks to achieve any goals in life, and accused her of trying to realize her failed ambitions through me. If you think I'm gorgeous,' she said drily, 'you should have seen my mother in her prime.'

'I take it they didn't get on?'

'No.'

'And you were often the one in the middle?'

'Yep. Anyway, when this modelling offer did come my way, I took it.' She looked rueful. 'All those classes must have paid off because I was flooded with more offers; my mother was thrilled, and even my father was happy for me. And it was fun to an extent although much harder work than people realize. There was also,' she spread her hands, 'a dilemma for me in that there was, is, a studious side to me and sometimes I couldn't believe it was really me, strutting my stuff down a catwalk in all these gorgeous clothes or wearing Versace against a background of Kakadu, for example, for a photo shoot.'

'So I was right about the steel-trap mind? Let me guess—a straight-A student?'

She looked rueful. 'Almost.'

'Let me also guess,' he said and watched her narrowly for a moment, 'that's when the high-life began. The champagne and roses, wealthy men, the races, your acquaintance with five-star island resorts and the like?'

'Yes,' she said simply. 'But, contrary to what you have suggested, there has only been one man in my life in that way.' There was also a challenging little glint in her blue eyes now.

But Bryn Wallis didn't apologize for anything. He said instead, 'He must have done an awful lot of damage.'

'What he did do,' Fleur said evenly, 'was appear to fall in love as much with me as I did with him. We were together for a year.' She shrugged. 'What I gradually discovered was, we had quite different expectations of where it would lead.'

'Marriage, six kids?' Bryn hazarded. 'Whereas he wanted a perpetual glamour girl on his arm?'

'Precisely.'

'Are you telling me you're gorgeous, studious and— seriously—a contented little homebody all at the same time?'

Fleur stared at him for a long, fraught moment and then she stood up. 'I don't know why I'm telling you anything,' she retorted crisply, and put her hands on her hips. 'Why should you find that so hard to believe?'

His gaze travelled up her bare legs, took in the curve of her hips and swell of her breasts beneath her shirt and shorts and finally arrived to clash with her own. 'I could be the same kind of man.'

'You certainly…you confuse the life out of me,' she said frustratedly. 'One minute you're trying to help, the next… Oh, what the hell!' She picked up her towel and costume and marched away.

He wasn't far behind her. 'Watch your step, Fleur,' he advised. 'This path is tricky at the best of times and shouldn't be marched over in a temper.'

No sooner had he said it than she lost her footing and collapsed in a heap. But she sat up almost immediately to drag her tumbled hair out of her eyes, which were blazing.

'Fleur.' He knelt down beside her but she interrupted him.

'If this is one of those…situations out of a romance novel where I've conveniently sprained my ankle and you…have to pick me up and clasp me to your manly chest, I'll…I'll scream!' she threatened furiously.

Not a muscle moved in his face but his eyes were a different matter. 'Do you have a sore ankle?' he asked gravely.

'And don't you dare laugh at me either, Bryn Wallis!' she commanded.

'I'm not—'

'Oh, yes, you are! I can see it in your eyes.'

He allowed himself the faintest smile then was all seriousness. 'Uh…should we just concentrate on any injuries you might have sustained?'

She gritted her teeth.

'What say I just help you up?' he suggested.

She started to protest that she didn't need any help but he picked her up and set her on her feet. 'How's that?'

She put her full weight on both ankles, one of which *was* sore, to her disgust, but, after testing it for a few moments, not that sore, she discovered. 'I'll be OK,' she told him.

He grinned crookedly down at her. 'What a pity. Although I'm not seriously wishing a sprained ankle on you, and, to be honest, I'm relieved on another front.' He looked up the headland. 'Clasping you to my manly chest is one thing but carrying you over that would be quite a task. Not that I wouldn't be capable or *manly* enough to do it,' he assured her, 'but it would be quite a task.'

Fleur set her lips but they refused to stay set. Hard as she tried, she couldn't escape the humour of the situation, as she had set it out and he had contributed to it. 'It's not funny really,' she said. 'I mean, I just…' She stopped and had to laugh.

And it happened again, they were laughing together then they were kissing each other. In a warm and friendly way at first. He kissed the tip of her nose and remarked that one of the things he liked about her was her sense of humour. She replied that it was impossible not to have a sense of humour around him! He laughed and put his arms around her to hug her—and that was when it started to turn serious.

They sobered and stared into each other's eyes and she knew she couldn't hide what being in his arms did to her. To feel the length and strength of his legs against hers, the hard muscles of his diaphragm against her slim figure, to be able to drink in his dynamic masculinity, through all her senses, even her pores, was too much to withstand. She simply couldn't resist when he started to kiss her deeply. She could only kiss him back fervently.

Nor was she helped by the fact that she had no underwear on beneath her shorts and T-shirt—it had seemed pointless to put on her costume beneath her clothes. So there was nothing to hinder his fingers as they explored her breasts, nothing to stop him touching her nipples and sending shivers of rapture through her as they rose to twin aching mounds, so sensitive that she sighed with a mixture of pain and pleasure.

But she wasn't alone in being vulnerable to physical delight. As often, Bryn wore no shirt, and she found that it was not only intoxicating to her to trail her lips over the smooth tanned skin of his shoulders, to allow her fingertips to twirl through the coppery curls on his chest, but also caused him to breathe unevenly and hold her even closer. He cupped her hips and she slipped her hands around his neck and tipped her head back.

He kissed her throat and she opened her hands and slid her palms down his chest. He released her hips and moved his hands, beneath the elastic waist of her shorts, to the most secret, intimate part of her. She gasped and her eyes widened but he continued to kiss her throat, and she slid her hands round him to smooth them up and down the long, powerful muscles of his back, and to quiver throughout the length of her at what he was doing to her as wave after wave of exquisite sensation ran through her.

'Take it off, your T-shirt,' he said barely audibly against the corner of her mouth, at the same time as he gave her a brief respite, which made her bite her lip on the urge to tell him not to stop—anything.

'I...' She couldn't go on and she closed her eyes, completely swamped by the powerful effect he was having on her. And she withdrew her hands from his body, crossed her arms protectively over her at first, then found the hem of her T-shirt, and pulled it off over her head.

He stared down at the delicate skin revealed with a faint tracery of salt on it, at the perfection of her breasts with their unfurled velvety tips, and kissed her deeply. Then he slipped one arm around her waist, holding her into him but allowing her to tip her head back again. She did so, and his lips moved down her throat towards her breasts, like a trail of fire. And that most intimate exploration of her commenced again at the same time as he tugged each full nipple in turn with his teeth.

She made a small husky sound that was halfway between despair and joy, then she gasped again and shuddered in his arms as he held her hard to him, and she felt him shudder too.

They stood like that, together, breathing as one, until she opened her eyes at last and her lips parted to allow one word to escape. 'Don't...'

'Only when you're ready,' he murmured.

But it seemed to take an age for the sensations to subside within her. When she sighed at last he picked her up, took her back down the track and walked straight into the sea with her.

CHAPTER FIVE

WHAT have I done?

The words ran through Fleur's mind more than once during the day. But what was she to think, she wondered, in the strange aftermath to such passion that had overwhelmed them equally?

They had floated side by side for a short distance then climbed out of the water and, by mutual, unspoken consent, started up the path again. The sun had been well above the horizon and her clothes had started to dry on her body.

Bryn had given her his hand several times to help her over the rough patches and there'd been consideration and concern in his eyes when she'd stumbled a couple of times. He'd steadied her gently and asked her if she was ready to go on. He'd even looped her tangled hair behind her ears a couple of times, and wiped the sweat off her face with his towel when they'd paused to catch their breath. So that she still felt so physically close to him, but they'd said nothing to each other about what had happened between them.

Then Clam Cove had come in sight, and she'd thought they must pause and somehow put into words their feelings. But no words had come to her, or to him. And halfway down they'd seen Tom on the beach waving to them energetically and starting up the path towards them...

'Why didn't you take me with you?' he demanded when they met up.

'You were asleep, old man,' Bryn said to him.

'You could have woken me up!' Tom pointed out aggrievedly. 'If you were going to wake Fleur up, why not me too? I hate being left out of things.'

'I didn't wake Fleur up. She didn't know I was going over the headland.'

'Didn't you, Fleur?'

'No, Tom. It was just a coincidence.' With devastating consequences? she wondered. Was there to be no communication between them at all?

'Oh, well,' Tom shrugged philosophically then grinned impishly. 'I forgive you this time! Bryn, don't forget, we're having a clean-up-the-garden day at school today and you promised to come and help.'

'For my sins, so I did,' Bryn murmured.

'Would you like to come too, Fleur?' Tom asked. 'Mums *and* dads are coming!'

Fleur looked over his head to his father as the implication of Tom's words hit her. To see her own shock mirrored in Bryn's eyes for a moment. Then he blinked and said to Tom, 'Fleur has her own work to do, mate, so we won't bother her. She's also got a sore ankle.'

Tom put his arms around Fleur's waist. 'You poor thing,' he said. 'I'll walk you to your bungalow. Do you think that stuff you rubbed on me when I had chickenpox will help? There's some left.'

Fleur's face softened and she went to stroke Tom's head but stopped herself. And she tried to say lightly, 'Thanks for the thought, Tom, but I'll be fine! You two had better get on your bicycles! I'll see you when you get back.'

Fortunately, there was plenty to do for the rest of the day.

Julene's special evening that she'd promised the diners of the previous evening's disaster was to take the form of a luau. Eric dug a pit for the fire over which a pig was to be roasted. Trestle tables were set up on the beach with colourful cloths, and Fleur spent her lunch hour helping to make leis.

'I'm wearing a sarong,' Julene announced. 'So should you,' she said to Fleur. 'We want them to feel like castaways on a Pacific island.'

'Sounds nice but I don't happen to have one.'

'I'll lend you one! Sarah and Rose are happy to wear them.' Sarah and Rose were the waitresses engaged for the evening. 'And Eric is going to wear a lap-lap.'

Fleur smiled. 'Well, I guess I can't let the team down. What about Bryn?'

'Bryn will wear whatever he chooses. It's no good telling him what to do or wear.' This was said with something of a bite in her voice because there were times, despite looking over the fence, as she had admitted to once, when Julene did not see eye to eye with Bryn and it required Eric to keep the peace. She shrugged, however, and went on, 'But I've got a lap-lap for Tom. There!' She surveyed the pile of leis. 'I think everything is under control—and there's a full moon tonight. Avail yourself of it, kid, if you've got any sense.'

Fleur blinked. 'Do you mean me?'

'Yep. Give him some of his own damn medicine. You in a sarong with flowers in your hair and around your neck, with a full moon—no better way to show Bryn Wallis a thing or two!'

'I...I'm not sure I know what you mean.'

Julene reached across to pat Fleur's cheek. 'Honeychild,' she said affectionately, 'you just let him know that if he wants you he's going to have to come clean with you. See, take Eric, now; he's like an open book, he's just straight up and down, but Bryn is a different matter altogether—he's much more complex and *driven*. You only have to look at all the things that bug him to know that!'

Fleur raised her eyebrows heavenwards. Only a couple of days ago Bryn had thoroughly enraged the shire council with a letter to the local paper detailing to the last cent how their salaries had gone up in direct proportion to how services on Hedge Island had declined—she had been the one to field all the irate phone calls.

'Damn!' Julene continued, looking past Fleur. 'Talk of the devil, there they are now! Bryn and Tom. Bryn told me this morning this could be all my show and he'd be happy to take orders, but that's like asking a tiger to be a good little pussy cat! I was hoping they'd stay out longer.' She marched off militantly.

Fleur stared after her with an involuntary smile on her lips but a frown in her eyes. Come clean about what? she wondered. And how to handle an evening beneath a full moon wearing a sarong and flowers in the company of a man who had, that morning… She stopped her thoughts deliberately, and stood up to return to her office. The movement caused her to wince slightly as she put some weight on her ankle, but almost immediately she welcomed that little tremor of pain.

In the normal course of events, it wouldn't be enough to stop her doing much, but who was to know that? So she had the perfect excuse to miss the luau, and fully intended to use it…

*   *   *

'There's the sarong, Fleur!'

Julene popped into the office at about four o'clock, to add, 'Now promise me you'll pick some flowers for your hair! By the way, Tom mentioned your sore ankle—should have told me earlier but I've got the perfect stuff for it.'

She produced a tube of anti-inflammatory cream and an ice pack. 'And anyway, all you're designated for this evening is to be guest liaison officer and all you have to do is sit around, talk to the guests and look beautiful! So hop off to your cabin now, rest the ankle with the ice pack on it and we'll see you around six. That's when everyone is coming!'

And she popped out, full of energy and determination.

Fleur looked at the sarong, a lovely silky concoction in a pale ice green with vivid pink flowers on it, at the tube and the ice pack, and swore beneath her breath. Talk about being outgunned, not to mention having her mind read, she reflected bitterly.

At half-past five, she reluctantly started to get ready.

She'd slept for half an hour, and had a visit from Tom, who was delighted with his lap-lap and full of excited anticipation.

'They've put up fairy lights in the trees and they're going to play music,' he told Fleur. 'Bryn's rigged up the speakers from the CD player on the beach and they've put down a dance floor. This is going to be a damn good party!' he added.

'Tom,' Fleur murmured, hiding a smile, 'I don't think you're old enough to use that kind of language.'

He wrinkled his nose at her. 'I heard Eric say it.'

'Eric is a lot older than you are.'

'Does that mean it's not *wrong* but you've got to be twenty-one or something to say it? Why? I know I can't drive a car because I can't reach the pedals, so that's a good reason, but I don't understand this.' He looked to her for enlightenment.

'I hear what you're saying, dude,' she replied. 'A lot of things kids are not allowed to do are because they're not big enough or strong enough or it might stop them growing. But swearing, you see,' she paused for inspiration, 'well, some people believe that swearing is not good for anyone, it's just not nice. That's why kids are discouraged from it. But when you're grown up you can make up your own mind about it.'

Tom thought for a bit then shrugged. 'If it's good enough for Bryn and Eric, it'll probably be good enough for me, when I'm grown up. OK, I'll wait until then. Oh, I forgot!' He ran onto the veranda and returned with a bucket of hibiscus and frangipani blooms. 'Julene said these were for you!'

At five to six, she stared at herself in the rather inadequate mirror. Her hair was loose with one flower pinned in at the side. She'd tried tying the sarong several ways and opted for a halter style and wore a swimsuit underneath. She was just about to put the lei round her neck, when footsteps sounded on her veranda.

'Knock, knock,' a voice said—Bryn's. 'Are you decent?'

She hesitated and her hands tightened on the lei, crushing some of the flowers. She put it on anyway and said, 'I'm just on my way down—if you've been deputized to come and get me. You go on; I won't be a moment.'

But he appeared in the doorway. 'I've brought you a drink.'

She looked across at him and swallowed. As Julene had predicted, it was no good telling Bryn what to wear. He had blue jeans on and a freshly pressed khaki bush shirt. His hair was brushed and he was neatly shaved. There was no bandanna, no pirate shirt, no attempt to look as if he were a castaway on a south-Pacific island. This was yet another Bryn, a stranger. He also had two glasses in his hands.

'I…' She stopped helplessly.

'I thought we could do with some Dutch courage,' he said and came in. 'You look beautiful—but then you always do,' he added, with his gaze lingering on the shine of her hair, the sheen of her lips and the satin gloss of her neck and bare shoulders. He came up to her to hand her a glass.

She hesitated then took it and turned away.

'I never did get you another chair.'

Fleur took refuge in her drink and discovered it was a brandy and soda. She waited for a moment after the first sip then turned back to him, avoiding his eyes. 'I really don't need one.'

He studied her bent head then touched the flower in her hair. 'Is it too late to say that I just—don't know what to say?'

She looked up fleetingly. 'Perhaps that says it all? So there's no need to—'

'There's every need.' He slipped his fingers beneath her chin and made her look up again. 'What would *you* like to say?'

Her eyes were very blue with just a hint of the sheen of tears. And her voice was low—but level. 'You quoted John Donne this morning. ''Go and catch a falling star'' is another line from that song. If that's what happened this morning, it slipped through our fingers because it's not the right time, or place, or we're not the right people for each other. That's all.'

His fingers were hard on her chin for a brief moment, and then his hand dropped. 'Very poetic,' he commented drily.

She shrugged, a delicate disclaimer of the charge. 'You started it.'

'Can't you forget him?'

Fleur's eyes widened, then she veiled them with her lashes. 'Perhaps no more than you can forget her.'

'If you mean Stella—'

'No, Bryn,' she said. 'I mean the one person that...you can never get out of your heart whether she deserves to be there or not, whether she was taken from you in other circumstances—however. I mean Tom's mother.'

He froze.

'I'm sorry,' she said huskily. 'But I do understand. Should we,' she raised her glass, 'finish these and join the party?'

But the party came to them in the form of Eric. 'Bryn,' he called, 'Julene needs a hand, mate.'

'Tell her...' Bryn said roughly and took a breath. 'Tell her I'll be five minutes, pal.'

Eric could be heard departing.

'Tom's mother,' Bryn said to Fleur, 'hasn't got anything to do with this. Well, she *has* but—'

'Fleur, Bryn, people are arriving!' It was Tom this time calling from below the veranda.

His father said, 'Damn!' And drained his drink.

'I think you should refrain from swearing in front of your son,' Fleur murmured.

'Two points,' he retorted coldly although less audibly. 'He is not my son, and what the hell has it got to do with you?'

Fleur's mouth fell open and her eyes widened.

He smiled unpleasantly. 'Take that to the party with you to mull over, Ms Millar. I'd be interested to hear your thoughts on the matter—once we get this…luau out of the way, of course. Coming, Tom!' he called and left the cabin.

The evening passed in something of a daze for Fleur.

She did more than what was 'designated' for her. She circulated amongst the guests and tried to project a party spirit, she danced with Tom but was not asked to dance with Bryn Wallis. While he was a model of 'mine host' bonhomie throughout the evening, it took some accumulated knowledge of Bryn to know that just below the surface of all this good humour there prowled Julene's tiger.

Julene even commented on it halfway through the evening as she watched Bryn discreetly and fanned herself. 'So that's the way the wind blows,' she commented. 'Didn't take kindly to the ultimatum?'

'No, I mean, I didn't… Why didn't you tell me?' Fleur asked with some difficulty.

'What, love?'

'That Tom is not his son…'

Julene pursed her lips. 'He is officially. Bryn adopted him.'

'But he's the living image of Bryn!'

'With good reason. Didn't he tell you any more?'

'No!' Fleur said frustratedly.

'Well, I think I'll leave him to explain— Oh, no. Here comes trouble!'

Fleur looked around but didn't see anything unto-
ward at first. Just a happy throng of guests who had
eaten well and were dancing it off beneath the fairy
lights in the trees or wandering along the beach that
● was lit by romantic braziers. Then she saw her—Stella,
also wearing a sarong and flowers in her hair, weaving
her way through the dancers towards Bryn.

He was talking to a couple but Stella went right up
to him, put her hands around his face and drew his
head down so she could kiss him. Surprise, Fleur
mused, could have accounted for his lack of resistance
to this—he'd had his back to her as she'd approached.
Surprise could not account for what followed, she reasoned.

Stella then positioned Bryn's hands on her hips, put
hers round his neck and danced him onto the floor.
Where she swayed in his arms provocatively, said
something to him that drew an, admittedly, reluctant
smile from him, but then he shrugged, kissed her hair,
and they began to dance together with evident enjoy-
ment.

Fleur turned away, held up a hand as Julene went to
say something and murmured, 'Don't. There's just too
much to cope with in relation to Bryn Wallis. I'm going
to bed.'

She had no idea how long she'd been asleep or what
woke her up, but as her eyelids fluttered open her first
thought was that she'd left the light on. Then the flick-
ering shadows on the walls, seen through the mosquito
net that veiled the bed, told her it was the oil lamp not
the electric light, which she had not even lit let alone
left on.

She sat up and looked around to see Bryn sitting in

the only chair. Her lips parted incredulously. 'What are you doing here?'

He seemed to rouse himself from a reverie. 'I was thinking that you looked like a princess, untouchable beneath that veil, even composed and reserved as you sleep.'

Fleur cast aside the net and was about to cast aside the sheet then remembered that all she wore was a short ivory silk nightgown with shoestring straps. But she did say tautly, 'Don't start that nonsense with me again, Bryn Wallis! And don't ever come in here again without my permission!'

'More and more like a princess,' he remarked wryly. 'Do you know you have the most elegant and fastidious nose, Fleur? I must say it lends itself beautifully to your regal air.'

'You...' Fleur paused and frowned suddenly. 'What...what on earth has happened to you?'

'Ah, you noticed!' He looked gratified and raised a hand to touch his right eye, which was darkened and half-closed, gingerly. Then he looked down at his dirty shirt, his grazed knuckles and the tear in his jeans. 'I got on the receiving end of a rather punishing left hook; I don't know if you know what that means—'

'Of course I do—you got punched!' Fleur broke in disbelievingly. 'Don't tell me *Stella* punched you!'

'Stella did not. What happened was, the guest I gave such a colourful come-uppance to last night—as you had tutored me in the art so expertly—returned tonight, nursing a definite grievance.'

Fleur's jaw dropped.

'As you say,' Bryn commented. 'Fortunately, everyone else was gone, Tom was in bed, so were Julene and Eric. I was just checking that all the braziers were out when he arrived unheralded and took me by surprise.'

Fleur closed her mouth and her lips quivered. 'What,' she said in a strangled kind of way, 'did you do to him?'

'Well, I took a little bit of purely defensive action, not being sure whether the guy had come to murder me or not,' he gestured as if to claim innocence of any real aggression, 'when I gathered, from his comments, that the one thing he could not forgive was being made to look a fool in front of his wife. Now that hit home. We men have—'

'Don't tell me, I know all about it,' Fleur broke in. 'Go on, what happened then?'

'I stopped—purely defending myself, of course— and offered him a drink.'

'Purely defending yourself, of course!' Fleur agreed gravely then could help herself no longer. She started to laugh. And she said unsteadily, 'Did he accept your offer?'

'He did. And we thrashed the whole matter out verbally and came to the conclusion that we were equally at fault, so we shook hands and parted on most cordial terms.'

'I see.' Fleur's voice was still unsteady. 'How many drinks did it take to thrash it all out verbally?'

'If you think I'm drunk, I'm not. Not precisely,' he corrected himself. 'It could even be that I'm only reeling from a particularly difficult evening on all fronts as well as the effects of some solid blows to the head.'

She eyed him suspiciously. 'So—were you hoping I would leap up and get a piece of steak to apply to your eye as well offering to bathe your cuts and grazes?' she enquired. 'I mean—is that why you came here, invading my privacy, and, what's worse, while I was asleep?'

'Heavens above, no, Fleur!' he marvelled. 'That'd be like asking a leopard to change its spots.'

'Just what do you mean by that?' She looked at him dangerously.

'Like asking you to come down from your lonely mountain peak of—'

'Shut up, Bryn,' she commanded. 'Oh, all right! Stay here.' She got up swiftly, reached for her terry-towelling robe and padded out of the bungalow.

Ten minutes later she came back with a pot of strong coffee and the first-aid kit.

She filled a bowl with water and Dettol and reached for the cotton wool then stopped to study him. 'Your hair is full of sand, you're grubby, bloody and probably sweaty—what you really need is a shower before I do this!'

'Are you asking me to totter back to my bungalow, survive a shower and totter back here?'

'A shower would probably sober you up— Oh, have it here! I'll go and get you some clothes.'

'Pyjamas would be appropriate,' he said.

'I'll get whatever *I* deem appropriate,' she retorted.

He grinned crookedly and replied meekly, 'Whatever you say, ma'am.' He hauled himself up out of the chair and stepped unsteadily towards the bathroom.

Fleur bit her lip, suddenly wondering if he was suffering from a concussion more than alcohol.

While she was getting his clothes she checked on Tom, to find him sleeping peacefully. But she gazed down at him for a few moments, completely baffled. If he wasn't Bryn's child, whose was he? And how come he was so like Bryn?

She shook her head and stole out, to run back across the sand to her bungalow. Bryn was already out of the shower, he'd poured the coffee and was sipping his, and all he wore was a towel tied around his waist.

'Here,' she thrust the bundle of clothes at him, shorts and T-shirt, 'get dressed then I'll fix you up.'

Sheer amusement glinted in his hazel eyes as he regarded her over the cup. 'I hesitate to contradict you in this forceful mood, Fleur, but there are places you would be unable to reach if I was dressed. You're not—shy, surely?'

Oh, yes, I am…

The thought flew across her mind, taking her by surprise but was nevertheless true, she knew, as her nerve ends tingled beneath the impact of his big, bronzed body even though it was slightly battered and he had a black eye. None of that altered the grandeur of his physique or made any difference to her memories of what had happened between them on the beach. None of it stilled her leaping senses as she remembered what he'd done to her and the sensations he'd brought alive in her…

She looked away and cleared her throat. 'All right. Turn around and I'll start on the back of you. However, anything that's under the towel you do yourself.'

'Of course,' he agreed as he obliged. 'That would definitely be above and beyond the call of—duty,' he added over his shoulder.

Fleur gritted her teeth and didn't respond. She found a cut on his shoulder blade, a scrape down his side and a graze on his elbow. She swabbed them carefully then dabbed on iodine.

'Turn around.'

He turned slowly. There was a long scratch down his upper arm, an angry bruise on his chest below his shoulder and the knuckles of his right hand were grazed. Without looking into his eyes, she dealt with his grazed knuckles. Then she looked at the scratch on his upper arm and, abruptly, she turned away from the clean, pure man scent of him and the urgent desire to put her arms around him and press herself against all that splendid physique.

'Fleur?'

'I think you can manage the rest,' she said barely audibly and reached for her coffee. 'I didn't get a piece of steak; you'd probably be better off with an ice bag for your eye anyway.'

He watched her narrowly as she inhaled the coffee aroma then sipped some with the kind of concentration one devoted to a lifeline…

Nor did he comment until he'd dealt with the scratch himself and paid another visit to her bathroom to change into the shorts and T-shirt she'd brought for him. Then he poured himself another cup of coffee and retired to the chair. She was sitting on the bed.

He said, 'Let's start at the bottom.'

Her lashes lifted and she sent him a startled little look.

'I mean,' he explained, 'on a scale of what's least important. Stella came to say goodbye tonight. She's leaving for her new post tomorrow, and she wanted there to be no hard feelings.'

Fleur said nothing but she couldn't mask the sceptical expression that lit her eyes briefly.

He shrugged. 'You're right. She also proposed that

we not lose touch and that there was no reason not to…take up where we left off from time to time.'

This time Fleur's expression was cynical.

'You disapprove?' he suggested.

'Not at all. It has nothing to do with me.'

'It has plenty to do with you,' he replied with irony. 'But we'll leave that for the moment. Tom,' he said, 'is my sister's son.'

Fleur gasped.

He grimaced and went on. 'Like you, Alana was gorgeous. The moment I saw you I was reminded of her; she had the same colour hair, same style, blue eyes.' He paused. 'But now that I've had time to think about it, I realize it's not so much a physical resemblance, it's that certain air that comes from deportment classes, acting classes, elocution and all the rest of it. She went through them all like you. She modelled, she dabbled in acting.'

'So,' Fleur said confusedly, 'the reason you took one look at me and decided you didn't like me was because I reminded you of your sister? I don't understand…' She shook her head.

'Let me finish. She also dabbled in life in the fast lane. She attracted men like bees to a honey pot, but what none of us realized was that her sophistication was only a veneer. When I did realize it, it was too late; not that I was home a lot but when I began to see the road she was going down I felt…responsible. Not a damn thing I did was any help, though. That's why,' his eyes were utterly compelling, 'when I sensed another girl going through something similar in you, Fleur, I thought it was what I needed like a hole in the head.'

Fleur was stunned for a moment, then there was genuine concern in her expression. 'What happened to her?' she asked quietly.

Bryn noted the concern and thought for a moment before he continued. 'When she discovered she was pregnant to a man who dropped her like a hot cake, she spent most of her pregnancy having psychiatric counselling. But when Tom was born she abandoned him to my mother and fled overseas, where she still is, seeking—' he stopped and sighed '—spiritual solace in another religion.'

'But,' Fleur whispered, 'he's such a darling…'

Bryn sat forward and stared at the floor. 'I know, and I still live in the hope that one day she will come back and be able to love him and let him love her, but it doesn't seem likely. She didn't even return when my mother died, although I have to say in her defence it was so sudden that she couldn't have got here in time. That's when I adopted Tom and came to live here. He was only three and, although my father loves him dearly, he would have had to rely on nannies et cetera to care for him.'

'And that's why Tom always calls you Bryn—I thought it was just a cute habit,' she said helplessly. 'Does he know all this?'

'Some of it. He knows he's different because he doesn't have a mother but until now it hasn't seemed to bother him. He is only six and he's had plenty of love and care. From here on, though, now he's started school particularly, I'm sure the anomaly of his situation is going to loom larger. He demonstrated that only this morning. But until he gets really anxious about it, well,' he shrugged, 'to be honest I don't quite know how to handle it, but the way he's taken to you…' He stopped and shrugged.

Fleur swallowed.

'By the way,' he said with a faint smile, 'you were right. I should not swear in front of children.'

Fleur echoed his smile but distractedly. 'And I reminded you of *all* this that first day?'

'Fleur, a girl like you wanting to bury herself on an island as an accounts clerk, which is virtually what the job is— Yes, you did. The only difference is, Alana chose religion. She dropped right out, in other words, but I knew you were also dropping out.'

'I see,' she said slowly. Then, 'But you dropped out yourself, Bryn.'

'That's the other problem I have,' he said and paused. And there was something very sombre in his eyes when he raised them to her at last. 'I hope to heaven I have never been responsible for the kind of misery Alana went through—'

'You must know whether you have or not,' she broke in.

'Do I? Sure, I know I haven't sent anyone into retreat, I know I haven't fathered any fatherless kids but,' he gestured with some frustration, 'I've never come across the one woman I knew I could spend the rest of my life with. And it came home to me very recently that, yes, I may have dropped out. Yes, I turned my back on the fast lane that I thought had been so disastrous for Alana, but I was still…looking for the kind of woman who was as little into the lifelong commitment as I was—Stella, for example,' he said drily.

'So,' Fleur groped for the right words, 'you see yourself as a "love 'em and leave 'em but leave 'em with a smile on their faces" type?'

'Thanks.' He grimaced. 'Even at two o'clock in the morning your steel-trap mind is functioning well, Fleur.

No,' he raised a hand to forestall her, 'you're right. But, as Stella demonstrated perhaps, I'm losing my judgement. Or, what's worse, I had done it before and not known it.'

'I see.'

'That's,' he looked at her wryly, 'not a steel-trap reply, Ms Millar.'

'Then perhaps this is,' she countered. 'I think you're trying to say that, like your sister, I'm desperately looking for love, or was, and got battered in the process by the kind of man you are yourself?'

He drew in a breath and something almost savage glinted in his eyes for a moment. Then he murmured, 'Once again I'm suffering from the "it's OK for me to admit these things but not so OK for you to agree" syndrome. That's it in a nutshell, however. It's also complicated by Tom's growing affection for you, Fleur.'

'Then I better pack my bags and go tomorrow, Bryn,' she said.

He stood up abruptly. 'Damn it, why don't you put up a fight?'

She blinked. 'You've just told me—'

'I've tried to explain why I'm...in some difficulty with you, Fleur Millar. All I've had from you is a watery version of one man's failings! There's got to be more to it than that.'

She shot up off the bed. 'Then how about I tell you about my failings, Bryn? I should have known! He was divorced, he already had children, he'd been through all that and was not about to go through it again. But I didn't see it. And when I finally came to my senses and broke it off I was tempted to...to give as good as I had got, and I did for a while.'

'How?'

Her eyes blazed. 'No, I didn't sleep with them, Bryn, but I went out with a few men, trying to be the party girl, the always sensationally dressed social girl they seemed to want, the girl they'd be happy to be seen with in the society pages. But it always came back to one thing—not one of them was interested in the real me; all they wanted was my body. And, what was worse, I started to realize how easy it was to move from one man to the next, looking for real love, perhaps just as your Alana did, Bryn.'

He closed his eyes. 'So you retreated.'

'I retreated. Too late, as it turned out, or,' she shivered suddenly, 'who knows?'

'What do you mean?'

'If you'd really like to know why I wanted to bury myself on your miserable island, I was being stalked. I...'

She stopped as, to her horror, hot painful tears were choking her.

'Oh, Fleur,' he said on a despairing breath, and took her in his arms, 'why didn't you *tell* me?'

CHAPTER SIX

'TELL me about it,' Bryn said gently.

Fleur was lying in his arms on the bed, where he'd taken her and simply held her until the paroxysm of tears had subsided.

Then she did tell him, gradually reliving the sense of claustrophobia, of always looking over her shoulder, the frustration, the fear and all the rest of it.

'Did you go to the police?'

'Yes, but it's like fighting a shadow. He never showed himself, I didn't recognize his voice, they had no idea where to start. He used to send me flowers but he used a false name when he ordered them. He used to ring me from a phone box and tell me what he'd seen me doing but it was always something dozens of people could have seen. He never threatened me, all he said he wanted to do was talk to me but...' She shivered.

'Go on.'

'So I moved, I changed my job and got a silent number. A month later he rang me at work.' She sighed. 'It was only a few days after that that your job came up. That's why...I really wanted it.'

Bryn moved restlessly. 'What about your parents? Couldn't they have helped?'

'For the first time in years, that I can remember, they're really close to each other. My father had a minor stroke but it seemed to bring them both to their senses and they decided to go overseas for a year. I think they're really happy travelling the world and I didn't want to bring them home with something I *thought* I could cope with.'

'How did they take your affair with a divorcée?'

'They weren't that happy about it but they didn't know how... I mean, I managed to persuade them I was fine when it ended.'

He reflected on this for a moment then he said, 'I should have thought of that,' he said. 'I should have tied it up. I did sense how eager you were to get the job. I did suspect you were running away from a man, but not a stalker...then you stopped biting your nails. And you never seemed to want to leave Clam Cove. Why couldn't you have told me, Fleur?'

'At the interview?' She shook her head. 'Who wants to take on that kind of problem with an employee?' She smiled tearfully. 'There were enough things you didn't like about me, anyway.'

He grimaced. 'Well, later, then?'

She breathed unevenly. 'I don't know. I didn't even want to think about it. I had started to feel so safe here.'

'You are but there's one way to make you even safer... You need a protector, Fleur. Here's what I propose. That we just do it.'

'Do what?' she queried, smiling faintly because this was Bryn Wallis at his most 'in charge'.

'Get married, have six kids, spend the rest of our lives not hammering things to death but living the undoubted attraction we have for each other.'

She raised her head and looked at him quizzically. 'That's sweet and I know I should have expected the kind of solution only you could propose but I also know you're not serious, so—'

'On the contrary, I am.'

'Bryn?' she whispered, stunned.

'I've made up my mind, Fleur,' he warned. 'Look, I know you love this place, right?'

'I… How do you know that?' she asked dazedly.

'I see a deep sense of contentment in you at times, when you're bird-watching, for example. When you're looking at the gardens as if you would love to get in and do some gardening yourself. When,' he paused, 'it moves you to swim in the nude because it's so beautiful.'

She rubbed her cheek on his shoulder and sighed. 'Yes, I do. But—'

'Then there's Tom—'

'No, Bryn,' she sat up, 'please. If Tom were your son and motherless I—' She stopped suddenly.

'That would make it all right?' he said quietly. 'Fleur, do you know what kind of an admission that is?' he asked intently.

She closed her eyes and he pulled her back into his arms. 'Tom has got to be told something soon, and all we can tell him is the truth, but should Alana ever come back we can never lose Tom entirely. And despite what I said, I don't think the fact that he's not my son is going to change the way you feel about Tom. After all, I am his uncle.'

'How much harder is it going to make it for Tom, though, if she does come back?'

'It's never going to be easy for Tom,' he said. 'I don't even know what will be harder for him—a mother who suddenly reappears in his life or one who doesn't. But we can always give him our love and support.'

Fleur said nothing for a couple of minutes, then, 'I can't believe I'm even having this discussion with you,

Bryn. You just don't marry someone because they're being stalked.'

He looked down at her, at his most enigmatic. 'You think that's all there is to it?'

'Not that long ago you were telling me you've never found a woman you could contemplate spending the rest of your life with.'

'Not that long ago I was fighting you, Fleur, for all sorts of reasons. As you were fighting me. But I think, each in our own stubbornness, we overlooked the most important thing of all. This.' He took her chin in his hand and drew the outline of her mouth. 'We have made exquisite love to each other without even doing it. If you know what I mean.'

She searched his eyes at the same time as some delicate colour rose to her cheeks.

'We have,' he said barely audibly, 'been united in an act so special and we were so stunned that we couldn't find one damn thing to say about it, and it wasn't even the final act between a man and a woman. We, Fleur Millar, are united whether we like it or not.'

'Like that, yes,' she said unsteadily, 'but—'

'But me no buts. Let it speak for itself.'

'Bryn,' she said on a breath, 'have you no idea how impossible this is?'

He smiled faintly and untied the sash of her robe. 'Tell me that later.' He freed her from her robe and slid his hands beneath the wisp of silk that was her nightgown. She trembled as they roamed over her body and knew she should resist what was to come, but the truth was, she couldn't. Because there was no pleasure on earth like the pleasure Bryn Wallis brought her, no rapture to equal it. And there was no way, she discovered, to tell herself that she hadn't fallen in love with this often difficult, sometimes funny and charming, always fascinating man—and believe it.

But did that mean what he felt for her was the same?

Then she arched her body beneath his hands, and could think no more. He slipped her nightgown over her head and kissed her breasts, tugging at her nipples with his teeth as he'd done before. And when that became too much for her he stroked parts of her body that she'd never before thought of as erotic, with the lightest touch until, mysteriously, she felt more desirable than she'd ever felt before, like a siren or a mermaid, celebrated and unique.

She ran her hands down his back because the need to give as she was getting overwhelmed her, and felt him wince.

'Oh,' she gasped, 'all your scrapes—'

'Forget 'em.' He looked into her eyes with those dancing glints in his good eye. 'I never felt better in my life.'

'You don't look it.'

'Then let's concentrate on you. I once told you you were competence personified. I was wrong. You're perfection personified. You're…exquisite,' he said unevenly.

'I didn't mean that; I just don't want to hurt you.'

'That should be my line,' he murmured. 'Does this…hurt?' He eased his weight on to her.

'No. I don't think you've ever hurt me less. I mean…' She stopped confusedly.

'I know what you mean.' He kissed her and slid his hands down to the tops of her thighs. 'How about this?'

She felt herself grow warm and wet beneath his touch as her breathing grew ragged and she moved sensuously. 'It's…heavenly,' she whispered. '*Bryn*—'

'Don't worry. I'm in the same situation,' he said into her hair. 'Dying, in other words.' And he entered her at last.

'Oh, thank heavens,' she breathed. 'It was so lovely last time but I think I would have died a little without…without…this.' But there was no need to say any more as he moved on her and the rhythm of their love-making claimed her deeply and powerfully and she had never felt more abandoned, more wanton, more willing to participate in the lovely act they were performing.

When it came, their release was the only road left to them and it claimed them simultaneously, taking them to a height that was a soaring explosion of pleasure.

'What was so impossible about that?' he said huskily and unevenly when they could speak again. He still had her wrapped in his arms, she was still trembling in reaction. And she tried to reply several times but couldn't frame any adequate words.

He kissed her then lifted his head to study her. 'You remind me of a flower, you always did, but more of a bud then. A slim cool mysterious bud whereas now you're a beautiful bloom. Say yes, Fleur. There's no other way for us to be now this has happened.'

Two weeks later, Fleur studied Bryn secretly.

His black eye had faded, his knuckles had healed and she knew for a fact that his other cuts and scratches were healed. And she thought, as she studied him, about life and how strange it could be. Two years ago she'd thought herself deeply in love with a man she knew well, and had longed for marriage and children with him. Two days ago she'd married a man she'd known for less than two months and about whom she knew very little. Well, she temporized, one thing she did know, when he set his mind to it she was unable to resist him...

It had happened because he'd laid siege to her in a way that had overwhelmed her. Snatches of it came back to her as she lay beside him and studied him secretly...

'We don't know each other well enough to get married, Bryn.'

'Nonsense, Fleur. You know exactly what I'm like! You've seen the worst of me—more than most, come to that.'

'But...' She paused.

'The other thing is, you handle the worst of me like no other,' he said with a crooked little smile.

They were sitting side by side on a log on the beach only hours after they'd made love and he'd proposed—if that was what you could call it. The sun was rising but there were high, feathery clouds in the sky promising wind and a perhaps less than balmy day. In fact, he'd raided his wardrobe after they'd realized it was a going to be a cooler day, and brought her one of his jumpers.

She pushed a far-too-long sleeve up and rubbed her nose on the back of her hand.

'And there's not much I don't know about you,' he continued.

'You never talk about yourself, though,' she said quietly. 'Julene reckons you're complicated and driven whereas Eric is like an open book and "straight up and down".'

He looked amused. 'What would you like to know?'

'Are you driven and, if so, why?'

He took his time. 'I was driven once. I used to report

wars. I used to think that if people knew the truth of things it might make it a better world. Then I realized that I was no better than the rest of us at finding and recognizing the truth. So I came here.'

'Had you planned to open a restaurant?'

'No,' he said ruefully. 'I planned to be a castaway fiddling around with bits of wood, being self-sufficient and being here for Tom. Then I found it wasn't enough, that I needed a challenge. I guess I inherited a cooking gene, so it seemed logical to think of a restaurant.'

'There are times, though, when I could swear you hate cooking for the public.'

He put his arm around her shoulders. 'There you are, you see. You do know me.'

'How long will that kind of conflict be…liveable, Bryn?'

'I don't know,' he said honestly. 'I do know I still love this place but it could be that we move on in the future.'

She trembled against him. 'You sound so sure we should do it.'

'I am.'

Two days later, she said to him, 'What are you doing when I see your light on in the early hours of the morning, Bryn?'

He looked surprised. 'Don't tell me we're two of a kind in that as well?'

'I… Sometimes I find it hard to sleep,' she confessed.

'So would I in your circumstances, but once we're married you'll never have to worry about that again. Mind you,' he said ingeniously, 'if our past record is anything to go on, sleeping may not always be top of the agenda for us.'

She smiled and coloured at the same time. He had just made love to her, and drawn an ecstatic response from her.

'OK?' he said and held her gently.

'Oh, yes.'

'So why did you blush?'

'Perhaps I feel a bit foolish. I...it's getting harder not to say yes,' she conceded.

'Good.' His eyes danced wickedly.

'You still haven't told me what you do in the dead of night,' she returned with some asperity.

'Ah. I decided of all the causes one could espouse,' he paused and it was almost as if he withdrew from her into another place, 'the abolition of land-mines would be the one I should pursue. So I write a lot of letters and articles, that's all.'

'I salute you,' she said very quietly.

He looked down into her eyes then drew her hard against him. 'Thanks. Will you marry me, Fleur?'

Something she couldn't identify stopped her in her tracks as she opened her mouth to temporize yet again. Something from an inner depth in him seemed to reach across to her, and suddenly she couldn't refuse to be reached. 'Yes...'

What was it, though, she wondered as she watched him secretly, that indefinable something that had reached across to her?

On the other hand, why she was unable to resist him was not nearly so obscure. She'd done the one thing she hadn't thought she was capable of doing again—she'd fallen in love. She could tell herself, she thought, that it had more to do with the protection he offered from the awful nightmare of being stalked. It was certainly a valid point. Even back here in Brisbane as they were, she felt totally safe with him.

But the fact remained that she had married him only knowing the bare bones of his background. She'd married him without telling her parents, who were somewhere in Mexico, but that was all she knew, and before she'd met his father—something she was due to do today.

Then Bryn stirred and his eyes opened. 'Why, Mrs Wallis,' he murmured, 'you're awake early.' And he pulled her from her position of watching him, with her head propped on her elbow, into his arms. 'What were you thinking?'

'All sorts of things,' she replied.

'You looked awfully serious.'

She shrugged and he kissed her bare shoulder.

'Don't tell me, let me guess,' he said gravely. 'You were wondering what the hell you've got yourself into?'

Her lips twitched. 'I was pondering the strange twists and turns life can take, yes.'

'Such as being here in the very hotel where we first met but in the Presidential Suite and in bed with a husband you barely know?' he suggested.

'It did cross my mind but how can you tell?'

'I've always been able to read you, Fleur. Did you come to any conclusion?'

'Such as?'

'Let me think,' he drawled. 'Is there anywhere else you'd rather be at this point in time? Is there anything you'd rather be doing than this?' He drew back the sheet and very slowly drew his hand down her body.

She tensed then relaxed with a sigh. 'At this point in time, Bryn? No.'

Something sharpened in his hazel gaze. 'You were thinking of resisting, Fleur?'

'Yes, but only momentarily,' she conceded. 'It occurred to me that you get your way with me far too frequently for it to be altogether a good thing. For your ego, for example.'

'Ah!' A wicked gleam entered his eyes. 'Well, if you seriously feel a dose of self-restraint would make my ego more manageable, I shall desist.'

'I doubt,' Fleur said, 'that anything would make your ego more manageable, Bryn. And you may,' she pointed out, 'have left it too late.'

'You can tell?'

'I can tell,' she agreed with a little gurgle of laughter.

'Damn. You're right.' He looked briefly glum. 'So what do you suggest? That you close your eyes and think of England?'

'Is that what you call desisting?' she countered on an indrawn breath.

'What would you call it?'

'I would call it extremely unsportsmanlike, Mr Wallis.' She quivered as his hands roamed about her with such familiarity.

'The thing is, I would hate above all else to have you...thinking of anything but me, Fleur.'

'Bryn,' she slipped her arms around his neck and kissed his throat, 'you win! Just don't talk nonsense to me any more, please.'

'It's true,' he protested. But he didn't say any more; there was no need.

*   *   *

They showered after their lovemaking then went back to bed and ordered breakfast.

Later, she said to him, 'Will this do?'

He was dressed in light grey trousers, a charcoal shirt and tie. The suit jacket hung over the back of a chair and he was working at a table, although she had no idea what at.

He looked, she reflected, light-years from the man she knew at Clam Cove. He'd had his hair cut when they'd arrived in Brisbane and it was now sleek and tidy. He was sleek and tidy and looked every bit the right kind of person to be able to command the Presidential Suite, a top executive perhaps, a man of wealth and power. The hotel even kept a wardrobe of clothes for him.

He turned as she spoke and raised an eyebrow at her.

It was a cool winter's day in Brisbane and in deference to this lunch appointment Fleur had had to buy an appropriate outfit the day before. She'd chosen a sherry-gold velvet suit with an ivory Thai silk collar. Her Cuban-heeled shoes were tan leather and she carried a matching bag. Her hair was wound into a pleat, she wore little pearls in her ears and a fine gold chain around her neck. Her make-up was understated and expertly applied and her perfume was light, with a hint of citrus.

He took his time before commenting. He studied her short, straight skirt and her long legs clad in the sheerest nylon. He took in the way her well-tailored jacket sat perfectly on her figure, her discreet make-up, his gold ring on her left hand, then his hazel gaze drifted to her hair.

'I think,' he said at last, 'I would prefer your hair down. Otherwise you are—gorgeous.'

'Why down?'

'Because I'm liable to spend this entire lunch longing to take it down and run my fingers through it.'

Her mouth curved into a smile but she said gravely then, 'Bryn, *I* think this is one occasion when you should practise some self-restraint.'

'Come here.' He held out his hand.

She walked towards him and he pulled her carefully down to sit on his knee. 'Have you any idea what you're asking?'

She hesitated and he fiddled with the chain around her neck. Then he laid his cheek against her breasts and inhaled luxuriously. She looked rueful and rested her chin on the top of his head. 'Are you not going to brief me about your father at all, Bryn?'

He drew away and looked into her eyes. 'Nope. You can handle him as you see fit.'

'I believe,' she touched his hair, 'you and he don't get along?'

'Who told you that?'

'Lyall.'

His eyes narrowed and were no longer bland. 'How did I come up between you and Lyall?'

Fleur traced the line of his eyebrow. 'He wanted to know how we'd met. I,' she paused and looked wry, 'could not resist asking him how well he knew you.'

'So you know a lot more about me than...than I probably realize?' He looked put out.

'Why shouldn't I?'

'Because you could have received all sorts of misinformation from a guy who doesn't know me that well at all; a guy, moreover, with a definite interest in you.'

Fleur took her hand away. 'Bryn, perhaps the most ridiculous thing about this line of conversation is that, for whatever reason, we're married now. Why shouldn't I know how you feel about your father?'

A look of thorough impatience crossed his face. '*I* don't know how I feel about my father,' he said savagely. 'Sometimes I admire him, sometimes he drives me up the wall. But what did you mean—for whatever reason?'

She looked blank.

'For whatever reason, we're married now,' he repeated.

She bit her lip. 'I...I... It just came out.'

'I thought we had the best reason in the world for getting married,' he said drily.

She freed herself and stood up. 'All right. No more questions.' She looked at her watch. 'Your father might not appreciate it if we're late for lunch.'

'Fleur—'

But she turned away and picked up her bag.

They said nothing as they travelled down in the lift; they didn't even look at each other.

Once again Bryn drew an immediate reaction from the staff as they stepped into the foyer. This time the manager himself hurried over and ushered them into the restaurant at the same time as he imparted the information that Bryn's father had just arrived himself.

She didn't have much time to take in the restaurant beyond a swift impression of beautiful flowers, lemon damask tablecloths, crystal and silver and soft background music before she was at a table and a tall, craggy, silver-haired man rose to greet her.

'So,' he said, shaking her hand and looking sharply

at her out of Bryn's, and Tom's, hazel eyes, 'you managed to nail him! Didn't think any woman ever would! You might have given me a bit more notice.'

'I'm afraid I was responsible for that,' Bryn said wryly. 'I was afraid she'd slip through my fingers, so I did the deed as soon as I decently could. Fleur, this is my father, Walter Wallis.'

'How do you do?' Fleur murmured and sank down into the chair that was pulled out for her.

The men sat and napkins were unfurled and placed on their laps.

'I hope he did do it decently,' Walter Wallis said to Fleur, 'and it wasn't some hippie kind of pot and flower-child affair.'

Fleur glinted him a quizzical little glance. 'On the contrary, he did it beautifully, Mr Wallis. We were married in the island church and we had a wedding lunch at Clam Cove, to which most of the local population of the island came. But I must admit I did have flowers in my hair.'

Walter Wallis pursed his mouth and regarded her critically. Then he turned to Bryn. 'I think I see what you mean.'

Bryn inclined his head but not before Fleur had seen the gleam of amusement in his eyes. It also occurred to her that the situation was bizarre. Here she was defending Bryn, when they had arrived at this lunch not talking to each other and with a pretty basic rift between them.

'Which is not to say,' Walter turned back to Fleur, 'that I approve of either of my children. I mean, would you? One of them is in an ashram, or whatever, the other buried away on a tropical island... By the way, what have you done with Tom and how did he take this turn of events?'

'Tom is with Julene and Eric Philips at Clam Cove. They very kindly offered to have him and some of his friends for an adventure weekend while we came down here for a few days. He was thrilled with the idea,' Fleur said serenely and accepted the menu she was offered. 'And Tom and I get along really well together.'

'I see.' Walter pulled a pair of horn-rimmed spectacles from his breast pocket. 'I can recommend the Moreton Bay bugs here. But, getting back to my children—'

'Do we have to?' Bryn asked. 'I'd far rather discuss the new hotel you're planning.'

'I would just like Fleur to know that you had every opportunity, you and Alana—indeed, you had a charmed, privileged upbringing—and now this!' He opened his menu but immediately closed it with a snap, as if his frustration was more than he could bear.

'Mr Wallis,' Fleur said, 'I can't comment on Alana but one thing I have noticed—your genes must be quite dominant. I see a lot of you in Bryn, and it's quite amazing how much Tom looks like you and Bryn.'

Walter Wallis looked gratified, although he said, 'And what's that supposed to mean?'

She shrugged and said quietly, 'In his own way, I'm sure Bryn is a son to be proud of. And that Tom will be a grandson to be proud of. They're very much like you, you see.'

Dead silence greeted this as a waiter poured champagne. Then Bryn raised his glass to Fleur and said, with something she couldn't identify in his eyes, 'For whatever reason, thank you for that, Fleur.'

Walter Wallis hesitated, then said, 'Don't know

much about you, my dear, other than that you're quite stunningly beautiful—you certainly turned plenty of heads when you walked in here, although no one would have expected less—but I like the way you conduct yourself.' He raised his glass to her. 'Welcome to the family.'

It was a much pleasanter atmosphere that saw them through the rest of lunch. It also provided some surprises for Fleur. Bryn may have chosen to bury himself at Clam Cove but it didn't stop him from being up to date with the Wallis hotel empire. Nor did it stop him from contributing some pithy advice on the new hotel being planned, to which his father at first took exception, but then gave in to the force of Bryn's arguments.

It also came to light that Walter had never been to Clam Cove, and the contact he had had with Tom over the last three years since his wife had died had been limited to visits when Bryn brought Tom down with him. It was when she suggested to Bryn's father that he come up to the island that the reason for all this emerged.

Silence followed her suggestion, a rather fraught silence, with Walter looking defensive and Bryn lying back in his chair, his hazel gaze steady on his father in a way that was loaded with irony.

'Oh, all right!' Walter said testily. 'I told Bryn when he came up with this damn-fool venture that I would never set foot in the place! That's why Tom has always come down to me, but that's not working so well now. I'd like to see more of him, so, with Bryn's permission, I may just avail myself of your invitation, my dear.'

'You're always welcome,' Bryn said quietly. 'So long as you don't lecture me or try to change me.'

'You're a hard man,' Walter commented ruefully.

'Funny you should say that; I can remember Mum saying the same of you.'

Fleur held her breath, then they both grinned.

'Well,' Bryn remarked as they got back to the suite, 'you charmed the socks off him—no mean feat. I'm just not sure why.' He hauled his jacket off, slung it over a chair and pulled off his tie. 'Considering,' he caught her wrist as she went to go past him into the bedroom, 'you weren't so charmed with me when we left here.'

'I'll tell you why,' she said evenly. 'Anyone with eyes in their head could see that you two are so alike, and so equally difficult at times, that there's bound to be friction between you. But, for whatever reason,' she paused and gazed at him levelly, '*I* was not about to become a cause of friction between you.'

He considered for a long moment with his eyes unreadable, his fingers hard at first on her wrist then relaxing. 'I think we should take this dispute to bed.'

Her eyes widened. 'No! If you think that every time we disagree, Bryn, you can take me to bed and...' She stopped frustratedly.

'Why not? There's a good old-fashioned saying about never letting the sun set on a quarrel.'

'The sun is far from setting,' she pointed out coldly.

'And we've only been married for two days.'

'Not a good omen?' She eyed him.

'I just didn't like that "for whatever reason",' he said and shrugged. 'To be honest, I didn't like to think of you discussing me with Lyall Henderson. If that doesn't give you good reason, Fleur, to know why I married you then let me show you.'

She frowned. 'Are you saying it makes you jealous to…?' She trailed off incredulously.

'Of course it does. Why do you think I was in such a lethal mood when he came to take you to lunch?'

She blinked dazedly. 'I had no idea.'

He smiled twistedly. 'You weren't supposed to.'

'Well…'

'That puts a different perspective on things?' he suggested gravely.

'Well—'

'You've said that,' he reminded her.

'I still don't understand…' She stopped and sighed. 'Perhaps I do now. Understand why you couldn't talk about your father.'

'So I'm forgiven?' He pulled her into his arms and nuzzled her neck.

'Bryn—'

He lifted his head. 'Just think of this, Fleur. In a couple of hours you've achieved what I've been trying to achieve for three years—getting my father to accept my way of life. What could you do for me in a lifetime?'

She looked into his eyes, saw the way they danced but also the query at the back of them, a query she was coming to know well, an unspoken question that was entirely intimate. Did she feel what he was feeling? in other words. She moistened her lips and for a moment wished she could say that she didn't. Because she wasn't sure that anything had been resolved or even what the issues were between them anymore. That she didn't know enough about him? But wasn't that something she could learn?

'I…am coming around to your way of thinking,' she said at last.

He smiled crookedly. 'Someone up there must like me, I'd be in dire straits otherwise.' And he started to undress her.

Later he said, 'Enough of this.' He sat up and ran his fingers through his hair.

She ran her fingertips down his back. 'If you remember, this was your idea.'

He twisted to look down at her, then bent down to kiss her and comb the glorious disarray of her hair with his fingers. 'I know but I can see the force of your argument—the one about self-restraint. We've only got two days in Brisbane—what would you like to do?'

Fleur yawned. 'I think you've worn me out, Mr Wallis. However,' she smothered a smile as he looked rueful, 'a nice soak in the bath might restore me. Then, I think I'd like to go to the movies, have a late supper, come back to bed, to sleep, of course—'

'Of course,' he agreed. 'Scout's honour! And tomorrow?'

Fleur thought for a bit then she said wryly, 'You may not approve of this but I'd like to get my hair trimmed, have a facial and a manicure, and go shopping.'

'So long as you spend some part of the day with me, why shouldn't I approve?'

'They're not exactly the pursuits of a dedicated alternative lifestyler.'

He laughed. 'They sound marvellously feminine, on the other hand. And it so happens I had some shopping in mind too. That we could do together.'

'Oh?'

'Uh-huh. I'm going to extend my—our—bungalow. It also came to mind that it's all very basic up there, apart from the restaurant, so I thought you might like to choose some things to make it more comfortable and homely.'

She looked surprised.

'Fleur,' he said, 'we may be drop-outs but we don't have to live in a hovel.'

For some reason a question floated through Fleur's mind. Will we always be drop-outs? She even parted her lips to say it then thought better of it.

'The other thing is,' he went on, 'I really don't expect you to go on working for me—'

'I don't mind. Wouldn't I be working *with* you, anyway?'

He kissed the tip of her nose. 'You're sweet. Thanks. But have you thought of what you'll do when the restaurant closes? Other than keep me happy and contented, of course,' he said innocently.

'Of course,' she agreed gravely then burst out laughing. 'That could be a full-time job!'

He gathered her into his arms. 'I love you when you laugh. But do you know what I mean?'

'Yes,' she said, still smiling. 'I need something like your woodwork to keep me occupied.' She paused and looked thoughtful. 'There are a couple of things I like doing. My mother and I used to make wall-hangings— a hessian background with tufted wool designs. I think the colours, the shells and the coral well, they've already made my fingers itch. And I could *use* shells and coral, bark and so on as well as wool.'

'Excellent,' he pronounced. 'We'll get all the stuff you need tomorrow. What was the other thing?'

'Don't laugh,' she warned.

He looked quizzical.

'I would like a piano—I have one, it's in storage, so

the only cost would be getting it there,' she assured him.

'Why would I laugh about that?'

'I don't know. I just felt as if I'd stepped out of that movie, *The Piano*. As if it was a rather bizarre thing to take to a tropical island.'

He grinned. 'So long as it doesn't produce the bizarre circumstances of that story, it's fine with me!' His eyes narrowed. 'You were going to say something earlier?'

She raised her eyebrows then shook her head. 'Can't remember.'

He looked at her intently for a moment longer but kissed her instead of probing further, to her relief. 'OK, let's get this show on the road!'

They dressed casually to go to the movies, saw a comedy and came out still laughing. Then they bought some fish and chips and went down to Riverside to watch the ferries plying the broad reaches of the Brisbane river as they ate their supper with their fingers.

Bryn was as good as his word when they went to bed and kept his Scout's honour, but it was also a rare pleasure to snuggle up against him and fall asleep in his arms.

There was a hairdresser and beauty parlour in the hotel, of which Fleur availed herself the next morning. Then she suggested to Bryn that, since she had clothes in storage as well as her piano, she should get them out instead of shopping to enlarge the small, rather dowdy wardrobe she'd taken to Clam Cove. But he disagreed, saying that all brides needed a trousseau, so they found a shop with summer stock available and he helped her to choose some light, colourful clothes.

He then directed her to the lingerie department of an exclusive store, and with a wicked glint in his eye recommended she let her hair down in the matter of sexy underwear. She pointed out that he spent a lot of time taking her out of her underwear, so mightn't it be a waste of money? He replied that, on the contrary, it only added to the pleasure.

They met again for lunch then went shopping armed with the lists they'd drawn up of the things Clam Cove needed to make it a real home. It was interesting to note, Fleur found, how their tastes, even in things like bed linen, coincided. It was also interesting to find that, unlike her father, who had left everything of that nature to her mother, Bryn had definite opinions and a connoisseur's eye for colour.

But when he suggested that she could do with proper office furniture she laughingly declined.

'Why not?'

'I really fought not to make a fuss about my office when you were quite sure I would,' she teased. 'It's…it was a victory to make it work and I intend to keep it that way. Besides, a lot of the charm of Clam Cove is the simplicity.'

He stared into her eyes. 'Thanks.'

The next day they flew home.

CHAPTER SEVEN

THEY'D been home about a week when all their purchases, and Fleur's piano, arrived in a container that had been shipped up the coast.

It had been a fun week. Tom was delighted to see them home, and still delighted with Fleur's new status. She and Bryn had debated the wisdom of explaining things to him thoroughly but had decided against it until Tom himself required some explanations. And, in fact, he'd said to Fleur that he knew she was not his mother so he would keep on calling her Fleur.

With Eric's help, Bryn had started the extensions to the main bungalow and the restaurant had run smoothly for the whole week, something of a miracle, as Fleur confided to Julene one day.

Julene laughed. 'That was one deeply frustrated dude, hon! It's no wonder we had a few spats and the like.'

Fleur looked away and a tinge of colour came to her cheeks.

Causing Julene to laugh again, indulgently this time, and pat Fleur on the shoulder. 'When it gets like that between a man and a woman, pet, there's only one thing to do. I'm glad you saw that.'

Fleur hesitated. 'There's still a lot I don't know about him.'

'It'll come! You'll see.'

What had come during that week was peace, accord and a lot of laughter between Fleur and Bryn as they relished being back at Clam Cove, and the weather was perfect.

Then their things had arrived and they'd all had a lot of fun unpacking and finding a spot for the piano, until Fleur discovered that all her possessions had been mistakenly shipped with the piano. Not that there was a lot, but all her clothes, books, CDs and odds and ends that she'd stored with the piano for her three-month stay at Clam Cove were now with her.

'Oh, no,' she said laughingly to Bryn as she wrestled open a large cardboard box, to see suitcases inside. 'All those new clothes! Oh, well, I'll be the best-dressed person on the island and I'm happy to have my books and music.' She looked up to disturb an unreadable expression in his eyes, unreadable except to say that there was something rather dark about it. 'What?' she asked, straightening and looping her hair behind her ears.

'You don't need those clothes.'

'I know! But now they're here…' She shrugged ruefully.

He studied her for a long moment then turned and walked away.

She blinked and was about to follow him but Tom raced up, having just discovered a brand-new bicycle amongst the other stuff. So she sent him after Bryn, whose idea the bike had been, to say thanks. Then Julene claimed her to wax lyrical over the new couch they'd bought for her and Eric's cabin, and Bryn and Tom returned, Bryn as if nothing had happened as he commenced lessons in how to ride a bike.

But Fleur was unable to dismiss the incident from her mind, so she closed the box up without unpacking anything and asked Eric to store it in the shed for her, saying she'd get back to it when she had more room.

It was a quiet evening in the restaurant that night and her services were not required, so she and Tom had their meal in the bungalow and then played Snakes and Ladders until it was time for him to go to bed.

Bryn came in at about ten-thirty to find her sitting at her piano but not even touching the keys.

'Something wrong with it?' he asked as he took off his bandanna and threw it across the back of a chair.

She came out of her reverie and shook her head. 'No. It's survived the move amazingly well. How did it go?'

'Like the well-run restaurant it is.'

A smile touched her mouth. 'You're very modest.' But she looked at him with a question in her eyes.

'I'm also knackered.' He yawned. 'Must be all the building I've been doing. Would you care to take me to bed, Mrs Wallis?'

'Bryn...' What happened today? The question hung on her lips now but she found she couldn't ask it. 'Of course.' She got up and stretched. 'I'm a bit tired myself.'

He looked around, at the things she'd unpacked, the colourful cushions, the painting they'd chosen together, the rug. 'You've done well. Still respectably "alternative" but not as spartan as it was. Would I be correct in thinking our new sheets et cetera are on our bed?'

'Yes.'

'Then let's road-test them.' He took her hand and, after the barest hesitation, she followed him into the bedroom. They undressed in silence with Fleur donning one of her new nightgowns, a black one with a lace panel down the front. She went to clean her teeth and when she came back Bryn was already in bed, lying on his back with his arms behind his head.

'They feel good,' he said of the sheets, 'and you look good. Come in.' She slid in beside him. 'Sadly, I'm unable to raise the energy to celebrate how good you look but I can—'

'Bryn,' she put her fingers to his lips, 'if you just want to sleep, that's fine with me.' And she arranged herself next to him, turned on her side facing away from him, and switched off the lamp.

About two minutes passed then she felt him sit up and heard him say, 'As you should know, Fleur, I don't take kindly to being gazumped. Do you know what that means?'

She sighed but didn't turn. 'I can guess—you don't mind telling me *you* don't want to make love to me but you do mind *me* agreeing with you?'

'Precisely. It…brings out the worst in me.'

'At least you can acknowledge that,' she said severely.

'It has also, on this occasion,' he continued smoothly, 'brought out the best in me, in a manner of speaking. Thus, I'm either going to have to make love to you or I'm going to have to get up and go for a long, cold swim.'

'Bryn,' she sat up abruptly, 'if this is another attempt to solve a dispute the way only *you* would conceive of doing…' She stopped frustratedly.

'What dispute?'

'Whatever it was that upset you about my old clothes arriving here!'

'Oh. That,' he said. 'What I'd really like to do with them is dump them in the sea!'

She gasped. 'Why?'

'Just in case some other man gave them to you, or you wore them for him, or they bring back memories.'

'You're not serious!'

'Sadly, I am,' he agreed. 'But I suspect I'm fairly average in that way. I mean, most men would rather not have their wives—'

'I bought every single item myself,' she broke in. 'None of them has any memories attached to them; I made a whole clean sweep when...' She stopped and bit her lip.

He took her hand and threaded his fingers through hers. 'That's OK, then. And I'm a bloody fool,' he said softly. 'Sorry.' He lay back and pulled her down with him. 'Let's see what I can do to make up for being such a fool.'

'Why couldn't you just tell me?'

He kissed her mouth and drew her hard against him. 'Because I didn't want to *sound* like a fool.'

'Before you go one step further, Bryn Wallis,' she said, 'I think we should make a pact. No secrets. If something is bothering you, tell me; and I will do the same.'

'Why not?' he drawled.

'I'm serious!'

'So am I. And you're even more gorgeous when you're serious.'

'I...you...you can't even *see* me at the moment.'

'But I can feel you,' he countered. 'Skin like satin, breasts—well, I can't even begin to tell you what they do to me and...ah, yes, especially when they do that.'

Fleur drew a ragged breath as her nipples peaked beneath his fingers. And she made a husky little sound in her throat that was a mixture of frustration and desire. But the frustration was no proof against what he did to her then, and what she found herself doing to him so that yet again they were united in physical splendour, and all else seemed to be mere trivia…

And things did get back to normal.

He himself retrieved the carton of her things from the shed and helped her to unpack. He also built a frame for her to hang the hessian from so she could start work on a wall-hanging. And they decided she would use her old bungalow as a studio, so he set it up there for her. He even displayed an artistic side by helping to create a design—on paper—to work from.

'You have so many talents, I'm amazed,' she told him as she studied the design they'd worked on together that blended the colour of the sky, the dark green of the hoop pines on the headlands, the sea and the riotous blooms in the gardens.

'I do,' he agreed.

'However, you're not exactly a model of modesty,' she pointed out.

'*False* modesty is not one of my failings, no.' He glanced at her, a model of seriousness.

'Bryn,' she started to laugh, 'you don't fool me! There is not a modest bone in your body.'

He looked hurt. So she kissed him and recommended that he leave her to do her own thing for a while in case she developed an inferiority complex. He did, and he left her studio severely alone for the next few days, but one late afternoon, as the sun set, he brought her a drink.

'How's it going?'

She stood aside to reveal what she'd done so far. He was silent for a moment then he said, 'Fleur, you could go into business.'

Her eyes widened. 'Do you think so?'

'Yes. We could hang them in the restaurant with a discreet "for sale" sign.'

'But this is rather an amateurish effort.' She stood back and studied it.

'I don't think so—it's lovely. It would stand out like a jewel on the right wall. Hey, you're a clever kid.' He handed her her drink. 'And a model of modesty,' he added with his lips quirking.

She sipped a deliciously fresh, chilled white wine. 'It's a funny thing. What started my mother off on this was a visit to Dunk Island and the artists' colony there. They do wall-hangings, pottery and so on. And now I'm on an island doing it.'

'Another of life's strange twists and turns,' he commented wryly. 'I'm sincerely sorry to have to ask you this, but Rose has a problem with one of her kids. Could you fill in for her tonight?'

'Of course! And you don't have to be sorry.'

'All the same, I am,' he remarked obscurely then changed the subject. 'Have you heard anything from your parents?'

'No. I've been e-mailing them once a week but they must be somewhere out the back of beyond where they can't access it.'

'So they still don't know we're married?'

'No. I just couldn't break it to them via e-mail,' Fleur said ruefully. 'As we agreed, Bryn.'

He nodded. 'I just wondered if you'd changed your mind, that's all.'

'I'd have told you.'

He put an arm around her shoulders. 'I wish I could whisk you away to a private dinner for two somewhere.'

She leant against him. 'What say we have a private nightcap on the beach later?'

He ran his fingers up the back of her neck and through her hair.

'Sounds nice.'

'In which case, I'd better go and get ready for work.' But she didn't move. Instead, she said, 'Are you OK?'

'Fine. Well…' He sighed.

'This is a night you don't feel like cooking for the public?' she suggested.

'Yes.'

'By my calculations there's only another month to go, Bryn, before the restaurant closes for the summer. Then you'll be as free as a bird!'

He laughed softly. 'OK. Let's go to work.'

So they did but, although they did have their private nightcap on the beach and when he took her to bed he made exquisitely tender love to her, she couldn't discard the niggling feeling that something more was bothering him. She hardly had time do more than ponder it, however, because the next evening three unexpected guests arrived for dinner at the restaurant…

Rose was still having problems with one of her children, so Fleur was waitressing again rather than disrupt the roster, when who should arrive but her parents, with Walter Wallis following on their heels.

'Mum! Dad!' she gasped. 'So that's why I wasn't getting any e-mails— Oh, no, I mean…Mr Wallis! Goodness me! I don't—'

But her mother was hugging her, then her father, and they were saying that they were staying at the resort because they'd decided to surprise her, and she was looking wonderful…

Which was when Walter Wallis took his turn to hug her, and comment at large that marriage to his son must be agreeing with her.

'*Fleur*,' her mother whispered, her gaze dropping to the ring on Fleur's left hand, 'what have you done?'

And her father went white.

Fleur looked around a little wildly and Bryn, who'd been standing arrested as he took in the scene, came down to introduce himself.

'Mr Millar, Mrs Millar, I'm sorry this must have come as a bit of a shock. I'm Bryn Wallis. Fleur and I got married a couple of weeks ago.'

Her mother's mouth dropped open as she took in the bandanna, the colourful outfit—and the butcher's apron Bryn was wearing. She turned to her daughter incredulously. 'You married a chef? Oh, Fleur!' And tears started in her eyes.

'Ma'am,' Walter Wallis intervened with dignity, 'he may look like a chef, not to mention a drop-out or a castaway or whatever, but my son will inherit a vast empire. Of course, what he chooses to do with it is another matter and a source of concern to me, I can't deny, but there's a lot more to him than would appear on the surface—at the moment.'

'Who cares?' Theo Millar retorted angrily. 'What I'd like to know is why he lured my daughter, my only child, up to this forsaken spot on the planet and persuaded her to marry him secretly!'

At this point Bryn glanced around, received a nod from Julene as she pointed in the direction of her bungalow, a signal to commandeer Eric, and he said quietly, 'Let's move this discussion somewhere more private.' He took off his apron and led the way to their bungalow, stopping only to pass the message on to Eric that his services were needed urgently in the restaurant.

Once inside their bungalow, her mother looked around incredulously, and gave way to her tears.

Several hours later, Bryn and Fleur were sitting on their favourite log on the beach sipping champagne beneath a bright white sickle moon as the tide lapped the beach rhythmically.

'Of course I don't think we're out of the woods yet,' Bryn said.

'Why are we drinking champagne, then?' Fleur asked.

He shrugged. 'We need some kind of a lift! At least your mother stopped crying.'

'I apologize for that.' She sighed. 'They've been away for a year. I mean, I knew it would come as a shock to her but not such a shock. I suppose I'm trying to say I thought that because they could do that, they would also assume I was adult enough to make... decisions like this.'

'Oh, a merchant banker, a stockbroker, a media magnate, for example, might have been a different matter.'

'Bryn,' she warned, 'she is my mother.'

'Sorry.' He sounded genuinely contrite. 'When it comes to that, your mother and my father make a good pair.'

Fleur smiled faintly. 'He did spring to your defence.'

'And there were some moments of high comedy.'

She looked rueful. 'Explaining Tom, for example, who slept through it all, thanks heavens? Yes.' It was at that point that her mother had called for a strong drink.

'What I would like to know,' Bryn said, after a long pause, 'is how you feel about it all?'

Fleur considered. 'Guilty for springing it on them like that. Guilty,' she looked at the glass in her hands, 'for underestimating the love and concern they feel for me—but not sorry I married you, Bryn.'

He drew her close and she felt him sigh deeply. 'Thanks for that. How do you think *they're* feeling now?' Her parents and Walter Wallis had returned to the resort.

'Still shell-shocked but, if I didn't entirely get through to my mother, I think Dad is reassured that I knew what I was doing.'

'Did you?'

The question hung in the air between them. 'Perhaps I had better show you,' she said simply.

He moved his chin on her hair. 'That's usually my line.'

'I must be coming around to seeing the wisdom of it.'

Her parents and Walter Wallis stayed for a week.

If Bryn had accused of her charming the socks off his father, she watched with some amusement as her mother's hostility crumbled beneath Bryn's charm and charisma at its most potent. Not only that, Walter turned on his own brand of charm for the duration of his stay. He was also genuinely intrigued by Clam Cove, Fleur could see, as well as see Bryn relax his defences on the subject. And Tom—well, Tom was just Tom.

You'd have to be a block of wood, Fleur reasoned, to be able to resist that kind of onslaught. Yet she had the feeling her father was another matter. She may have reassured him that she'd known what she was doing but she sensed that he had other reservations. And on their last day he suggested she walk along the beach with him, artfully consigning her mother to Julene.

Fleur knew something was coming and couldn't help herself from trying to pre-empt it. 'I know how hard this must have been to accept, Dad, but it would make me really happy if you could be happy for me.'

'I am, darling.' Theo Millar took her hand. 'But I don't imagine it's all going to be smooth sailing.'

Fleur looked across at him. 'Is it ever?'

He shook his head. 'No. I guess your mother and I are good examples of that.'

'That's one reason I didn't let you know,' Fleur confessed. 'I didn't want to spoil this time you were sharing in more...unity than I could remember.'

'Fleur, I know. And your mother will get over that. But I know Bryn Wallis, you see.'

Fleur stopped dead. 'How?'

'Oh, I'd never met him. But I used to read his columns and reports regularly. From places like Kosovo, Cambodia, the Middle East, Northern Ireland, Angola and East Timor. Then I read a report that his photographer—they'd been together for years—had been killed by a land-mine in Angola. From that day onward I never read another report with the Bryn Wallis byline.'

'I...I didn't know,' Fleur whispered.

Theo Millar looked concerned. 'It may not be something he can talk about, but,' he gestured to take in Clam Cove, 'it could be the reason for all this.' He paused. 'I guess what I'm trying to say, Fleur, is that I've sensed a couple of things, rightly or wrongly. One is that what you feel for him is not in question and therefore I *am* happy for you, darling.'

Fleur swallowed a lump in her throat. 'Thanks.'

'But I also think you've chosen a very complex man, and one who may have a lot of conflicting issues to resolve. It can put a lot of strain on a marriage.'

'Did you...' she looked into her father's eyes '...did you have those, Dad?'

'Oh, yes. Hopefully mine were not what Bryn has to deal with, but all the same... I fell in love with another woman when you were four or five. I chose not to pursue it but I couldn't forget it, and your mother sensed it. I often think that's why she was so insistent about trying to mould you into the person she would have been if she hadn't married me.'

'I'm...so sorry, Dad. But things came right for you and her?'

'Yes.' Theo looked into the distance and put his arm about his daughter. 'A little brush with mortality brought me to my senses and I found again the woman I had once loved enough to marry.'

'Don't let her worry herself about me, Dad,' Fleur said urgently.

'Fleur,' her father smiled wisely, 'I'll try. On one condition; I know there have been things you've tried to hide from us, for precisely that reason as well as,' he looked bleak for a moment, 'the friction it caused between me and your mother. But we are always there for you, and we're there united now. Just remember that, darling.'

'I think I need a holiday!'

They were standing on the jetty, waving goodbye the

ferry carrying his father and her parents, when Bryn made this pronouncement.

Tom was with them and he seconded the idea enthusiastically.

'Most of our life is like a holiday,' Fleur pointed out laughingly, to discover herself on the receiving end of an oddly penetrating glance from Bryn.

'True,' he said slowly. 'Perhaps we need to go and work down a coal mine for a change.'

'On the other hand,' Fleur paused, 'I was listening to the weather report this morning and they're forecasting a fifteen-knot south-easterly tomorrow. Good sailing weather.'

'Are you suggesting something, Fleur?'

'Uh-huh—it's Monday tomorrow, our night off. What say we persuade Eric to take the *Julene* out?'

'You're a genius, my dear.' Bryn possessed himself of her hand and kissed her knuckles. 'That's exactly what I need—a good, brisk sail.'

As it happened, what he got in a freak accident aboard the *Julene* the next day whilst they were raising the sails was a two-day stint in hospital on the mainland with some cracked ribs, concussion and a severely sprained ankle.

Nor was he a good patient, Fleur discovered; in fact he discharged himself against medical advice at least a day early, he commandeered a seat on a helicopter ferrying guests to the resort and turned up at Clam Cove out of the blue just before she was due to take the ferry across to spend the day with him, as she had on the two previous days.

He had a pair of crutches and his chest strapped and when she started to protest he propped himself against a wall, pulled her into his arms and said into her hair, 'Nothing on earth will make me go back! I also thought you might be pleased to see me.'

'I am! But I'm also worried about you! I've been a nervous wreck ever since it happened and we had to call out the coastguard because you were out like a light, and I didn't know how badly you were injured,' she said with a bubble of hysteria rising in her throat. 'And now you've just...walked out!'

'Hush.' He stroked her hair. 'I'm as tough as old boots, but it's nice to know you were really worried.'

'Of course I was,' she said indignantly. 'What did you expect?'

He laughed softly then winced. 'It's still nice. Unfortunately laughing, sneezing, coughing or anything of that nature is still a bit painful and I've been warned off sex for a time—'

'So I should think!'

'Mrs Wallis!'

'Bryn, you know what I mean,' she said ominously.

'So long as I'm still allowed to hold you, sleep in the same bed with you, that kind of thing?'

She softened at last. 'Be my guest,' she invited.

He kissed her. 'That's better. So. How has the old place got along without me?' He looked around.

Her lips curved. 'Admirably!'

He frowned. 'You don't say...'

'I do. Julene was inspired. Once again Eric came to the rescue and was her offsider. Yeah, it all went really well.'

'I don't like the sound of that one bit,' he commented.

She looked innocent. 'I thought you'd be pleased!'

'Pleased! You have just made me feel supremely dispensable, Fleur.'

'Oh, I wouldn't say that. There is a certain...*je ne sais quoi* lacking when you're not here.'

'Ah. I rather like the sound of *that*,' he replied gravely.

'I rather thought you might but—enough of this!' She released herself. 'Since you are back, there's one little person who has also been very worried about you. Come and say hi to Tom.'

It was a joyful reunion he shared with Tom. And things settled down once again, giving Fleur a chance at last to ponder her father's words to her.

Of course it hurt, she discovered, to think that Bryn had not been able to confide in her about his losing his photographer in such an horrific way, although it did explain why land-mines were his chosen cause. But was that the reason he had dropped out, she pondered, rather than Alana? And how long would he be happy living this life, she was forced to wonder as she remembered the odd times of discontent he'd exhibited.

She'd resolved none of these matters when, a week after he had come out of hospital, she woke up one night and he wasn't in bed beside her. She found him on the veranda, standing motionless. She switched on a lamp in the lounge and he turned convulsively, to stare at her as if she were an absolute stranger.

'Bryn?' She frowned and walked out to him to see that he was sweating and dishevelled. 'What's the matter? Your ribs? Your ankle?'

She saw him attempt to relax. 'No. Probably just something I ate.'

'You cooked everything you ate, remember? It was your first night back.'

'So I did. Perhaps I've picked up a virus.'

She hesitated, not entirely convinced. 'Come back to bed, then.'

'Fleur—would you mind if I dossed down on the couch? I'll probably toss and turn a bit and keep you awake.'

'Yes, I would mind. Just tell me where it's hurting and I'll get you something first, though.'

'It's…' He grimaced. 'Just a headache, really. I'll take an aspirin. And I will sleep on the couch, Mrs Wallis, so no arguments. Off you go!'

She went back to bed reluctantly, remembering what an awful patient he was and how he hated to be fussed over, but the next morning he appeared to be restored to normal.

'I wonder what it was?' she said to him over breakfast in the restaurant. 'I've checked with Julene and Eric, and Tom, and we're all fine, so it couldn't have been food.'

'I probably overdid things a bit, as you've frequently told me. But I'm fine now!' There was a certain determination with which this was said that caused her to think better of pursuing the issue any further.

So she shrugged. 'OK. Bryn, I really need you today.'

'How very gratifying,' he murmured and shot her a devilish little look.

'I mean,' she said severely, 'I'm about to finalize your quarterly BAS—Business Activity Statement,' she elucidated, 'for GST purposes, but we need to run through it together.'

'It will be my pleasure. Running through things with you is something I always enjoy.'

She eyed him suspiciously. 'This is serious, Bryn.'

He lay back in his chair. 'Haven't I mentioned before how much I like it when you're serious?'

A little tremor ran through Fleur as she was reminded of a certain conversation they'd had on the subject—and what had followed. She looked at him judiciously. 'I think it can wait for a day or so.'

'Why's that?' he asked lazily.

'Because I very much suspect…your intentions today.'

'You mean you've divined that once Tom has gone to school I have every intention of taking you back to bed and keeping you there for as long as I please?' he queried with a raised eyebrow.

She looked around hurriedly but no one was in earshot. 'Could that not be classed as doing too much?' she responded.

'Far from it. It could even be that seven days of living in celibacy with you may have benefited my ribs but not my sanity.'

She opened her eyes at him. 'Was that the problem last night? Why didn't you…?'

He laughed softly. 'I really don't know. Shall we do it?'

'I can't think why not.'

'This is deliciously decadent,' she said later as she lay in glorious disarray in his arms.

'Mmm,' he agreed. 'Fleur, there's something I need to tell you.'

She stretched and the sunlight coming through the

open shutter flickered up and down her body as it shone through a palm tree moving lazily in the breeze. 'Yes?'

'I need to go away for a couple of weeks. My father has to have an operation and he needs someone to hold the reins for him.'

She sat up and pushed her hair behind her ears. 'Oh. Not serious, I hope?' she asked with concern.

'No, but a knee replacement, which can be tricky.'

'That's a relief, Bryn, but couldn't Tom and I come with you?'

There was a momentary silence, then, 'I don't think it would be much fun, for either of you. I'd rather you stayed here.'

She turned to look down at him. 'This all sounds a bit mysterious and…unexpected,' she said slowly.

'You were the one who forged a closer tie between me and my father,' he murmured.

She frowned. 'Would you rather I hadn't?'

He sat up at last. 'No. By the same token, I can no longer ignore his plight, if you know what I mean.' He smiled briefly. 'One of us in an ashram, the other a drop-out on a tropical island. But the real reason I'd like you to stay here is…so that I can think of you like this, with sunlight and shadows on your beautiful body, waiting for me, calling me back like a siren…'

And he pushed her down onto the pillows gently so he could observe at his leisure, every inch of her and celebrate every inch of her until she was aquiver with desire and consumed by a need to give herself. She was taken in a way that reached new heights for them.

The next morning she drove him to the resort, where there was a private plane waiting for him on the airstrip.

She looked at it and felt a moment of sheer panic, which must have shown on her face because he said quietly, 'Fleur, you know you're just as safe with Eric as you are with me.'

'Yes, of course.' But that hadn't been her concern—the fear of being stalked had faded far into the back of her mind, to be replaced on this sunny morning by the sudden, irrational fear that Bryn would fly out of her life and never return. She swallowed and dredged up the routine she and Tom employed. 'Stay cool, dude.'

He responded in kind. 'Don't do anything I wouldn't!' And kissed her deeply before he got out and walked over to the plane, where the pilot was waiting for him. She waited until it had taken off then drove back towards Clam Cove. But on the crest of one of the hills there was a parking spot where you could pull off the road and enjoy the scenery. She did so and switched the engine off.

The surface of the sea was wrinkled today and there were white caps but it was a warm breeze blowing—a reminder that summer was just around the corner. Summer, she thought. How would she cope with summer when the restaurant was closed? More to the point, how would she cope with not knowing what her future held? With a husband who was growing more and more like a closed book to her?

She was not imagining it, she told herself. There was no real reason she and Tom couldn't have gone to Brisbane with him. In his first year of school a two-week break wasn't going to do Tom any harm, and with extra staff Julene and Eric were quite capable of running the restaurant.

There was no reason why she couldn't be told if his 'drop-out' life was starting to pall, or if that was why he needed something to pull him back to Clam Cove. Did he honestly think, she mused, she couldn't see, behind his occasional remarks, a restlessness in him? The day on the jetty, for example, when she'd pointed out that their life was like one long holiday and he'd replied that perhaps they needed to work in a coal mine for a while.

And what had really been behind his distress two nights ago?

The thing was, the thought came to her out of all this, if he'd married her, if the *real* reason had been because Clam Cove was losing its charm and he needed a diversion, she had failed signally to provide one.

'No,' she whispered. 'No…do I believe that of him? But it was so unexpected, it *was* something he appeared to be fighting against. Or was it even simpler—Tom needing a mother?'

She closed her eyes and sighed deeply as she thought about that, and wondered why he couldn't tell her about his life before Clam Cove? Or if he had any doubts that she hadn't fallen totally in love with him? So many things, and then the thought that she'd fallen for the wrong man twice now…?

'Eric,' she said a couple of days later, when she was helping him to unload the fresh catch of the day from the dinghy, 'did you know Alana?'

'Yes. Not very well but both Julene and I met her a couple of times. Why?'

'Do I remind you of her?'

Eric considered. 'Yes, at first. Now, not at all. And it was always hard to pin down.' He frowned. 'The way you walked perhaps, something…a little bit sad about you.'

Fleur winced inwardly and changed the subject. 'It must have been terrible for Bryn when he lost his photographer. Did you know him then?'

Eric straightened and regarded her seriously. 'Yes, I did. We worked for the same news agency at the time. I was part of the back-up team. Has he been having nightmares again?'

Fleur released a shaky little breath and closed her eyes. Of course, that explained it. She lifted her lashes. 'Yes, although he doesn't like to talk about it. How…how did you know?'

Eric gestured towards the main bungalow. 'I asked him once if he still had trouble sleeping because I used to see his light on sometimes. That's when he told me. I think it's an occupational hazard, if you've been in that line of work. I sometimes can't sleep. But I didn't go through anything like what Bryn did.'

Fleur studied the day's catch for a long moment. There was a nice haul of whiting, flathead and a couple of coral trout. 'Do you think he'll want to stay here forever?'

He shrugged. 'Julene and I were thinking of moving on, Fleur. But the other day he suggested we might like to consider caretaking the place during the summer. He didn't say why but it made me wonder.'

'Would you…consider that?' she asked, carefully trying to conceal the shock in her voice.

Eric looked around. 'Yes. We love it here, we could both get jobs at the resort and the more money we have put away, the better. But…' He stopped a little awkwardly. 'I guess you know more about his plans.'

'No,' she said barely audibly.

'Fleur—I don't know what to say.'

She smiled briefly. But could think of absolutely nothing to say herself.

That afternoon she got her usual call from Bryn, but it turned out to be a far from usual call because of the news Bryn had to impart, still sounding dazed himself about it. Alana had come back…

CHAPTER EIGHT

'Bryn! That's…that's wonderful!'

'Yes,' he said down the line. 'I'm still finding it hard to believe but it's the best news I've had for years.'

'Is she staying?'

'Yes. She says she's got herself together at last and she never wants to leave Tom again. She's dying to see him, although she's scared stiff at the same time because she doesn't know what to tell him and she feels so guilty—but I'm sure we can work that out. Dad, as you can imagine, is over the moon and it's the best tonic he could have at the moment. Fleur, will you bring Tom down? I'm trying to organize a flight for tomorrow.'

'Of course! What should I tell him, though? And where will they live…?' She paused and felt a little arrow of pain pierce her heart.

'Alana wants to come to Clam Cove for a time. Fleur, I know how much you love Tom—'

'Don't worry, Bryn,' Fleur said quietly down the phone. 'The sooner this happened, the better for Tom. It's going to be much easier for him to accept at this age and, if it hurts a little, I'm also tremendously happy for him, and her.'

There was a short silence. 'You are still his aunt.'

'That too!'

'Fleur, are you OK?'

'I just told you—'

'No,' he broke in. 'Look, I don't think you quite understood why I didn't want you to come down.'

She took an unexpected breath. 'Perhaps not. But I don't think we should worry about that at the moment. Getting this reunion right is the main thing. Bryn, if any pre-explaining to Tom is required I think you should do it. You're still the person he admires most on the planet.'

'All right, but so far as post-explaining goes, to you—'

'Later, Bryn,' she said quietly, 'I'm fine. Tell me more about Alana.'

He hesitated, then did so and they ended the call companionably.

But she was not fine, of course.

She went to sit on their favourite log on the beach, and stared unseeingly out to sea. She'd barely had time to get over the shock of discovering that Bryn had asked Julene and Eric to caretake Clam Cove for the summer without consulting her, she mused, before this news had hit her.

Not, she reflected, that she had married Bryn because of Tom. She could never deceive herself about that. But Tom had been a part of Clam Cove and its fascination for her. All that was due to change now and it would require an effort from her, that she would gladly make, to ensure that Tom had no conflicting feelings for her. But it mightn't be easy. Would it even be harder, she pondered, to be wondering if Bryn had married her *because* of Tom?

'It seems to me,' she murmured to the sea, 'that there's a growing list of reasons for why he might have married me, none of which was the right one. Tom,' she counted off her fingers; 'because I was being stalked; because he was restless and needed a diversion, which I patently didn't provide other than in bed. I just don't know what to do.'

'So we're going to Brisbane to see Grandpa?' Tom said. 'Yippee! Anything else I should know?'

Fleur regarded him affectionately at the same time as she thought, Help! 'Bryn has a surprise for you,' she said.

'Oh? What?' he asked excitedly.

'I can't tell you that. It wouldn't be a surprise then! But you remember meeting my parents, Tom?'

'Sure.' He looked at her enquiringly.

'Well, I may spend a bit of time with them. I'm their only kid, you see,' she said gravely.

'Can I come?'

'No, dude. But you're very important because you're needed to make your grandpa feel better after his operation!'

'Just don't stay away too long, Fleur,' he warned, then looked impish. 'Or do anything I wouldn't!'

Fleur relaxed inwardly. An hour later they stepped aboard the private plane that had picked up Bryn and were winging their way to Brisbane.

Bryn was at Eagle Farm to meet them and Fleur felt her heart start to beat heavily at the sight of him. He was wearing the same clothes as he'd worn the first time they'd met, although she wondered if he remembered that or if it had any significance—or if she was grasping at stray thoughts because she didn't know what else to think? Other than that what she planned to do was going to be harder than she'd expected.

Then she was in his arms and Tom was hugging

them both. Finally they turned and there was a tall woman standing diffidently behind them but with such a look of hunger in her eyes as they rested on Tom…

Alana Wallis was in her early thirties, willowy and, as Bryn had told her, she had the same colour hair as Fleur, although it was cut short, and blue eyes. She also had the same bearing that Fleur could recognize as being that of a trained model. But when she smiled you could see the relationship to Bryn, and to Tom…

It was Bryn who said, 'Alana, this is Fleur. Tom, I don't know if you remember me telling you when you were a kid that your mother, who was also my sister, had to go away? Well, now she's come home, for you, and here she is right here.' He put out a hand to Alana, gave Tom his other hand then piled all their hands on top of each other.

Done so simply, Fleur marvelled some time later. Although, it was only the groundwork, of course. Because Tom, being Tom, had had his own unique reaction to this turn of events.

He'd said to Alana, 'Hello! Do you think you're going to like me?'

Alana had cleared her throat and said simply, 'Yes. Very much. But you might like to take your time about getting to know me.'

'Well,' he'd considered, 'I might do that. Let's go and see Grandpa. Fleur told me I was very important because he needs me to make him feel better after his operation!'

'You're not wrong, old son,' Bryn agreed. 'Let's go.'

It was only after dinner that night that Fleur and Bryn were alone.

The Wallis family home in Brisbane was on Hamilton Hill with views of the river and Moreton Bay. It was a lovely old Queenslander with verandas all around and some priceless *objets d'art* within. It was at the same time, she couldn't help reflecting, strange to think that both the son and daughter of this house had shunned it.

She was watching the lights on the river, the rhythmic blinking of the red and green channel markers, the blue and yellow lights of the leads, lights she knew well, when Bryn found her on the veranda.

'I brought our coffee. Penny for your thoughts?'

She turned to him. 'I was thinking that you and Alana did well today,' she disseminated.

'Yes.' He put the cups down on a wrought-iron table and pulled up two chairs. 'We decided a low-key approach was the only way to go.

Fleur, what's wrong?'

She sat down and studied her cup. 'Bryn, I'm going to spend some time with my parents. Oh, I'll stay another day or so but I really think it will make it easier for them both, and easier for me. Tom knows about it and he doesn't mind.'

'I mind.'

Fleur raised her eyes to him at last. 'Why? Surely we should think of Tom first? I don't want him to be torn between me and Alana—'

'It can only help him to know that you approve of Alana, Fleur. But how is he to know that if you jump ship?'

'I'm not jumping ship,' she returned evenly. 'If I'd wanted to do that I would have done so by now. And I do approve of Alana. I know I've only known her a few hours but I think she's lovely, and brave, and my heart goes out to her.' For a moment there was a glint of tears in Fleur's eyes. 'But do you think I couldn't see her…anguish and guilt when it was me, out of habit, he wanted to read his bedtime story?'

'Fleur,' there was something grim in the set of his mouth, 'I know it's asking a lot of you, but only *you* can help Tom make this transition. Disappearing is not the way; gradually releasing the ties is.'

'I wasn't going to disappear,' she protested. 'It so happens my parents live half a mile away. I could see him every day!'

'How about me?'

'You too…'

'Is that what all this is about, Fleur?'

She picked up her cup and sipped her coffee. Then she could no longer lie. 'Yes. It's a funny thing, Bryn,' she put her cup down, 'but I feel as if I know less about you than I did when I married you. Which was not a lot at the time, anyway.'

'What do you want to know?' he drawled.

'Nothing,' she replied flatly, 'if that's the way you feel.'

'If you think your timing is good, Fleur, you're wrong. And if you're comparing me with Eric, no, I guess being an open book and "straight up and down" is not my forte.'

He closed his eyes abruptly and when he spoke again it was in a different voice. 'But it doesn't mean I want to be anything other than married to you.'

She stared at him, transfixed.

He opened his eyes. 'I came down here on my own because I needed to think things through. I told you that I could no longer ignore my father's plight but I'm still not sure whether I want to…take over, or going on living a lotus-eating life at Clam Cove. I was going to, when I got back, present all the pros and cons to you so we could make a joint decision.'

'Why couldn't you have told me this?' she asked huskily, at last.

He gestured. 'I don't know. There are some things I'm not good at, Fleur. Tearing you away from Clam Cove…has turned out to be one of them.'

'If we were together, would it matter? What do you mean?' she added immediately as the impression sank in that she had not grasped his meaning at all.

But they both turned at a small sound and it was to see Alana standing hesitantly in one of the veranda doors.

'Come and join us,' Bryn said immediately and got up to pull forward another chair.

'Thanks.' She had a cup of coffee in her hands. 'It's been quite a day. To be honest, it's been a turbulent few months as I came out of…six years of a kind of numbness. Fleur, you probably can't understand—'

'I can,' Fleur said quietly. 'As Bryn knows, I went through a period of wanting to withdraw myself.'

'You've obviously been wonderful with Tom,' Alana said after a moment. 'I don't know how to thank you and I can't help wondering how difficult this must be for you.'

Fleur could see again the genuine emotion and anguish in Alana, and she sighed inwardly, as she knew what she had to do, and would have had no problem doing if it weren't for Bryn and the doubts she had about their marriage. 'We can get through this together, Alana. I know we can.'

* * *

'Thank you for that,' Bryn said as he closed their bedroom door.

Fleur looked around, at the twin beds with their beautiful old mahogany headboards and padded gold quilts. She glanced up at the embossed pattern on the pressed-iron ceiling then walked across to the dressing table.

'I'm just wondering,' he continued, 'how you would like us to go on, Fleur?'

She sat down on the stool and picked up a silver-backed brush. She turned it over in her hand then stroked her hair with it. 'What did you mean about finding it hard to tear me away from Clam Cove, Bryn?'

He stared at her then sighed. 'You turn so many heads, Fleur.'

Her eyes widened.

'My father was right, the day we had lunch with him, but I see it again and again.'

'Would you like me to wear sackcloth and ashes?'

'No.' He shook his head. 'I know this is not particularly rational but…' He paused.

'Let's follow it through,' Fleur said huskily and put the brush down as she realized she was gripping it tightly. 'You still haven't changed your original opinion of me, have you, Bryn? You think that the more men I'm exposed to the more likely it is that I'll be tempted to run off into the "fast lane" again and become man-bait, too gorgeous for my own good and all the other things you've said about me.'

'Fleur, no—' But he stopped as she stood up.

'Then,' she said and couldn't quite stop her voice from shaking, 'there's the supreme irony that Tom no longer needs a mother, so you needn't have married me at all.'

'That's not true—'

'Oh, I think it might be.'

'Fleur,' he said harshly, 'your imagination is working overtime.'

'Think what you like, Bryn. You're not the one who had to be told almost everything she knows about you—secondhand. You asked me,' she swallowed, 'how I would like us to go on? I'll do all I can for Tom and Alana but I would like to be alone tonight.'

His mouth hardened. 'Be my guest,' he drawled and walked out.

The next three weeks were the hardest three weeks of her life, she was to think later.

By day, she and Bryn were as normal as possible, although anyone who took the time to think about it would have noticed that they were never alone together. On the other hand, it mightn't have been that noticeable because Bryn was also very busy, holding the reins of the Wallis empire for his father. But by night, they slept in separate although adjoining bedrooms with the door firmly closed between them.

It was inescapably the right way to go for Tom's sake, though, as Fleur poured her heart and soul into, very delicately, befriending his mother and loosening the ties. Not that it was a penance to befriend Alana. Once she began to lose her diffidence a warm, intelligent person emerged with touches of Bryn's sense of humour.

Fleur discovered that Alana had made the transition from her retreat three months previously so that she could come to grips with life in the real world before she tackled getting back to Tom. She also found out that Alana had discovered a vocation in life during her retreat. If Bryn had inherited a cooking gene and a way with wood, his sister could paint.

Of course it wasn't all plain sailing. There were times when Tom was fractious for no good reason, except that he could obviously sense there were changes looming in his life. It was on these occasions that Bryn, and his father when he came out of hospital, were invaluable. For that matter their transparent love for Alana and relief to have her back were also invaluable.

In fact, she said to Fleur one day, 'They're so good to me, I don't know why…' She stopped and sighed. 'I always used to think Tom was better off without me. That was my greatest hurdle and greatest pain. I still don't know how I came to have such little self-esteem.'

'I do,' Fleur replied. 'Because I went a little way down that road myself. What I thought was the love of my life…fell apart and it was a little while before I realized I was…looking for love and the more I didn't find it, the more diminished I seemed to feel. Is that how it may have happened for you, Alana?'

'Yes. Oh, *yes*! But you must have had a lot more sense than I did. And now you've got Bryn.'

'Now I've got Bryn,' Fleur echoed and forced herself to smile. 'I believe you're coming back to Clam Cove with us?'

Alana hesitated. 'I'm not quite sure what I should do. Clam Cove sounds ideal and Tom was obviously very happy there. As a matter of fact, Bryn suggested that we all go back together, Dad as well, while he's convalescing, but I wanted to be sure it was what you wanted, Fleur? Bryn,' Alana hesitated, 'doesn't seem altogether certain that his future lies there.'

Fleur flinched inwardly. 'I know.'

'So I wondered whether it was a good idea to take Tom back and then have to uproot him again if, for example, Bryn decides to sell it.'

'I see your point,' Fleur murmured through a bit of a daze that she devoutly hoped Alana didn't detect. 'Um...I did have a thought, Alana. Not in direct relation to Clam Cove but—well, you've met my parents? They don't live far away but I was thinking of going to spend a few days with them. It won't come as a shock to Tom because I mentioned that I might do this before we flew down. He was quite...cool about it.' She smiled briefly. 'The time has to come when I'm not there in his life and this may be a good way to...' She stopped and gestured. 'Do it naturally and not so that he feels he's being—'

'Torn away from you?'

'Yes. You know, I can see a growing affinity between you and Tom already, so—'

'I think that would be a good idea,' Bryn said behind them.

They both turned, Fleur convulsively, to find Bryn smiling down at her in a way that sharply reminded her of what Julene had once said of Bryn along the lines of—asking him to do anything he didn't want to do was like asking a tiger to be a pussy cat. Because she had never seen a more tigerish glint in his eyes beneath the amusement. And yet, this was not what he had wanted originally, she thought chaotically.

Then he ruffled her hair lightly. 'Something has come up. May I have a moment of your time, Mrs Wallis?'

It was to the bedroom she was using that she followed him. He held the door open for her politely then closed it and leant back against it. 'So you're still of the same mind, Fleur?'

She stood in the middle of the room in her simple white trousers and lemon blouse. Her hair was gathered in a scarlet scrunchie. 'You just said you thought it was a good idea.'

He shrugged. 'We might as well be living in different houses, so what's the difference?'

She swallowed.

'In fact it will probably be easier to maintain the fiction that this is a happy, loving marriage that way. I don't know about you,' he said with irony, 'but I am starting to feel like an actor in a very bad farce.'

'Bryn…'

'On the other hand, there's one way we could end all this. I'm talking about a time-honoured way that has worked for us before. If you recall.'

Fleur bit her lip but also discovered his words were like a hail of bullets tearing into her heart. Nor did he stop there.

'Last night I even wondered if I should try the…are you lonesome tonight, Mrs Wallis? routine. Then I thought that you were probably back in your ivory tower and sleeping the sleep of the just and the… righteous,' he finished softly but lethally.

Tears pricked her eyes. 'I never claimed to be either,' she said huskily.

He raised an eyebrow. 'I thought you had it all worked out to the last letter? In fact, I thought there might be only one reason why you hadn't walked out already.'

'There was,' she said, still battling tears but refusing to give in to them.

'May I set your mind to rest, then? Your stalker has been identified.'

Fleur's mouth fell open. 'How?' she whispered. 'Why?'

'How?' He grimaced. 'Money. A private-detective agency, in other words. From your résumé which I still happened to have, they tracked back through your last two jobs. From the address of the job you had before last, they did a search of the florists in the area. They found several that still had records of delivering flowers to you but once he got careless and paid for them by credit card. The name matched the name of someone who worked for the same corporation you worked for.' He told her the name.

Fleur sank down onto the end of one of the twin beds. 'I never knew anyone of that name.'

'All the same, that's how he was able to trace your address and phone number. Then—who knows?—he may have got lucky just ringing around similar corporations and asking for you.'

Fleur shivered.

'But you never have to worry about him again, Fleur,' he said quietly. 'Nor was it only you he stalked. He turned out to have a record of it, but in New Zealand—he was a Kiwi. He also suffered the...' he gestured '...misfortune of losing his life a couple of months ago in a motorbike accident.'

She exhaled slowly then she said dazedly, 'Why did you do that, Bryn?'

'I thought it should be done. I didn't anticipate being able to remove the fear of it quite like that but I was determined to make sure he never bothered you again.'

'Thank you,' she whispered and sat in silence for a long moment as she digested it all, and found herself wondering if the real reason he'd done it was so that he could release her from their marriage with no guilt about her being stalked… 'So now I'm free to go, in other words?' she said and looked at him at last.

'It would appear to be what you want.'

'What will you tell Tom and Alana?'

'Nothing at the moment,' he said flatly. 'Other than that you're visiting your parents for the time being.'

For a moment she was tempted to tell him the truth. That it was for Tom's sake that she'd stayed, not because she was afraid to leave him—she hadn't even thought about it. That this visit to her parents had not been planned as an attempt to leave him but to give Tom and Alana some time alone. And yes, to give herself a bit of a break, she couldn't deny, but also a chance to desperately think of a way round this impasse between them.

Yet now she had virtually been presented with no good reason to stay with him as he saw it, unless she was prepared to sleep with him again. And to gloss over again all the things she didn't understand about him, all the things it hurt her not to know. The biggest bar of all, however, she thought sadly, was that he had never changed his mind about her.

'Well, if you're wondering whether I'll fade away gracefully, Bryn, I will. I'd like to think there'd be no hard feelings because of Tom. But I don't want any of your worldly possessions, so perhaps you could arrange—things?'

They stared into each other's eyes and for a moment she remembered another time and place when he'd suggested she put up a fight… But almost immediately she knew she couldn't.

'That's all?' he said at last.

Only you can rectify this state of affairs, Bryn, she found herself wanting to tell him. But what was the good?

She stared down at her hands. 'It's been nice knowing you. It's been a real education at times, too. Would you tell Alana I'll go home this afternoon but I've got a headache, so I'm having a bit of a rest now?'

She heard the savage breath he took and tensed, not knowing what to expect. Then she heard the door open and close, and she was alone. That was when the tears came, and she stayed in her room for a couple of hours until she got the dreadful grief she felt under control. She also packed. When she did leave her room it was to find, courtesy of the housekeeper, that Alana had taken Tom for a ride on the Rivercat, which he adored. That Walter Wallis had been chauffeured to his physiotherapist and that Bryn wasn't expected home for dinner.

It was now or never, she thought. But she sat down and wrote Tom a note, reminding him that she was going to stay with her parents. She drew a funny picture of a mother goose wearing a bow around her neck, and a father goose with a collar and tie, both huddled anxiously around a gosling called Fleur. 'Stay cool, dude!' she wrote, and… 'Don't do anything I wouldn't!'

But although she rang her parents, and spoke at length to her father, it wasn't to her parents' home that she went when she left the Wallis mansion in a taxi.

CHAPTER NINE

SHE spent two days in a hotel, slept a lot, then she flew up the coast and took a ferry to Hedge Island.

The first thing Fleur noticed when the ferry came in was that the *Julene* was not on its mooring.

Discreet enquiries of the ferry captain provided the information that Eric and Julene had gone away for a couple of days on it; he'd spoken to them on the radio.

She breathed a sigh of relief at not having to explain things to them or beg them not to get in touch with Bryn. She had no doubt that Bryn would not dream she'd come back to Clam Cove, and no fear that he himself would come to Clam Cove in the next few days. She knew his father wasn't capable of travelling yet, apart from anything else.

So she hired a Moke and drove over the island, to find the gates shut and padlocked, and a notice on them that the restaurant was closed for the summer.

But she hadn't spent three months at Clam Cove without discovering certain things. Like the way round the fence line she'd come across on one of her rambles, and where all the spare keys were hidden. There was virtually no crime on the island anyway, so few people bothered to lock up at all—Eric and Julene would have had no fear of leaving the place for a few days. And she was able to drive the Moke in and relock the gates.

But as she wandered past the restaurant and onto the beach she asked herself why she had come. Ostensibly to collect her things but someone else could have

173

packed them up for her. No, she thought, it had been like a siren call to her soul to see Clam Cove one last time. It was as if only by doing this could she find the answer to why things had gone so badly wrong. It was the knowledge that without this answer she'd never have any peace of mind again.

But as the breeze lifted her hair and she looked around at the palm trees, the headlands, the sheen of sunlight on the sea, as she smelt the salty tang in the air and heard the murmur of the waves on the reef and the high, free whistle of a fish hawk, she thought she may have miscalculated. Because the memories held captive here at Clam Cove might be more than she could bear...

Bryn was everywhere. It was impossible to look at the restaurant, now so quiet and idle, without seeing him in his bandanna and pirate shirt, on the good nights when he was charming everyone witless, or the bad nights when you felt like throwing a glass of wine over him and had done so...

How could you forget Bryn and Tom conducting long serious conversations as the little boy fetched and carried for Bryn while he was woodworking, then breaking out into laughter and song?

It was impossible not to be reminded of his compassion and his humour, all the things that he felt so deeply about and some of the impossible situations he got himself into. She was standing on the spot where they had once laid a dance floor on the beach, and that night came back to her vividly. So typically Bryn, she thought, to pour cream, raspberries and wine over a man then end up trying to make amends because he'd insulted him in front of his wife, but of course there was so much more to remember about that night...

In fact, she crossed her arms protectively over her body as it all flooded back, trying to ease the pain as she wondered why she'd done what she'd done—left him.

Then, after an age, she forced herself to walk up the steps to the veranda of the main bungalow and another memory came back to her. Of a man in the grip of a nightmare that he couldn't even begin to tell her about. And she knew, for better or worse—she wasn't sure which, but all the same—why she'd done it. She just wasn't built to accept half a loaf from the man she loved... Otherwise she would have persevered, she thought with tears streaming down her cheeks. And she just wasn't built to be held in suspicion because of what had happened to his sister or because she turned heads.

It gave her some relief to think this, not that she hadn't thought it before, but it presented itself to her back at Clam Cove as the philosophy she should adopt to help her over the worst of leaving Bryn. It even had a name, she reflected. Go and catch a falling star... Whether any other woman would ever catch the falling star that was Bryn Wallis, she didn't know, but she hadn't been able to. How did you catch a falling star anyway?

The next morning—she'd spent the night on Julene's new couch—she finished her packing. Some of it would have to be sent on, including her piano, of course, but a lot she could take with her. Especially if she left her new clothes behind. It sent a tremor through her to think of discarding another set of clothes because of a man and she suddenly knew she couldn't do it.

So she packed each item, some of them that they'd

bought together, some she'd worn in the most intimate circumstances with him, carefully.

Then it was all done and she decided to go for a last swim at Clam Cove. It was a glorious day. Hot, clear and incredibly peaceful with only the sound of the birds and cicadas shrilling in the bush, the lap of the water to be heard.

She spent half an hour in the sea, swimming then floating on her back with her eyes closed and wondering how she was going to force herself to leave. When she came out she dried herself off and wrapped the sarong Julene had given her over her bikini. But she stood on the beach for an age before she could tear herself away.

She didn't see Bryn until she was almost upon him. He was sitting on the restaurant steps and it was as he stood up that she raised her eyes from the path—and stopped as if she'd been shot. He wore khaki trousers, a check shirt and deck shoes. She looked around wildly, to see another Moke parked beside hers.

'Hello, Fleur,' he said quietly.

'But…but…Tom…your father,' she stammered incoherently. 'How could you leave them? Why are you here? I thought I was *safe*…'

He closed his eyes briefly. 'I knew you were here.'

'You couldn't have,' she protested. 'I didn't even tell my father. I just said I was going away for a couple of days. And Eric and Julene aren't—'

'No one told me, Fleur. I…sensed it.'

Her eyes were huge suddenly. 'How?' she asked hoarsely.

He smiled drily. 'It was where I most wanted to be and I just had the…intuition that it was because you were here.'

'Bryn, what are you saying?' she whispered with her heart starting to pound.

'That it took losing you to…bring me to my senses,' he said sombrely.

'But I can't…I can't go through all that again.' She put a hand to her heart and her eyes were stricken. 'I've broken all the ties, I've—'

'I'm not asking you to,' he interjected. 'I just wanted you to know why I was the way I was. Look, I've brewed some coffee. Could we…talk?'

They sat on the veranda under an umbrella.

He poured the coffee. 'There's so much to say, I don't know where to start, but perhaps the accident on the *Julene* will explain some of it.'

Fleur blinked.

'I hate hospitals.' He grimaced. 'They're probably not places you're supposed to enjoy but my memories of them are especially horrific. I had a friend and colleague killed in a land-mine accident. They tried their hardest to save him but the facilities were primitive. Even so, all hospitals have certain similarities. Losing him in any accident would have been bad enough but the horror and the futility of that—well, hospitals will always bring it back to me.'

She gazed at him with her lips parted, then collected herself. 'My father told me—he read about it. And Eric…suggested you might be having nightmares about it again.'

'What else did Eric tell you?'

'Just that he'd been there too… Is that why you discharged yourself so soon?'

'Yes.'

'But you couldn't tell me at the time, Bryn?'

He fiddled with his spoon and she noticed the lines scored harshly beside his mouth. 'Fleur—and I've never told *anyone* this—that awful accident was why I came to Clam Cove in the first place. Yes, Alana and Tom fitted in with it. But it was the only way I could deal with the guilt I felt.' He looked up abruptly. 'If I hadn't been so determined to get that story, it mightn't have happened.'

She drew in a shaky breath. 'Oh, Bryn. And you've been living with it ever since?'

'Not only that but the feeling of being...cauterized. As if all the things I saw had closed off any finer feelings I possessed. I truly, for example, did not believe I could fall in love properly—until you came into my life. I didn't believe I had any real emotional depths left—except for Tom—and I was happy to be that way.'

He looked around then continued very quietly. 'That it should be you to bring me out of it, a girl who reminded me of my sister and her downfall, a girl who would always turn heads, was the added irony of it and it undoubtedly added to my cynicism. That's why I fought falling in love with you, Fleur. Or, it was one of the reasons.'

'What others were there?'

He shrugged. 'I've told you about Alana. But, even after I'd acknowledged what was happening to me, something you yourself said stayed with me. Something about the one person you can never get out of your heart whether they deserve to be there or not. When you believed Tom was my son you thought it was Tom's mother I had in my heart. Ever since I've wondered how true it was for *you*, though, to say it in any context.'

'Bryn—'

But he put a hand over hers. 'That's why I hated the thought of you wearing clothes he may have bought, or ones that brought back memories of him. And even when I discovered that they weren't, I had to grapple with the fact that your break-up with him, a man whose name I don't even know, was so traumatic, you couldn't bear to be reminded of it. That's when I began to suspect I would only feel safe here at Clam Cove with you.'

She was silent.

'So,' he said, 'I don't know if it makes any sense to you or if you even want to hear the rest?'

'Tell me,' she said barely audibly.

'If I gave you cause to believe I married you because Tom needed a mother, what actually happened was, I couldn't bear to think of you being lonely and frightened and I used any tool I could think of to get you to agree. The one thing I couldn't bring myself to do was admit that I was back in touch with my emotions—and as scared as hell that I could get hurt because of it.'

She wiped her eyes with her knuckles and sniffed.

'Not only back in touch with my emotions,' he went on, 'but experiencing the one emotion that had eluded me even before I got all bitter and twisted.' He smiled painfully. 'In other words, I'd fallen deeply in love with a girl in a way that had never happened to me before. A girl, moreover, who was sworn off men.'

'Oh, Bryn,' she said, and her voice caught in her throat. 'Yes, I had sworn off men but...' She stopped helplessly.

His hand tightened over hers. 'Tell me your side, Fleur. Please.'

She looked at him for a long time with all sorts of

emotions chasing through her eyes, which were, he thought, as blue as the ocean, while her hair had dried to a tangle of fairness.

She cleared her throat at last. 'Every way I turned, I seemed to come up with a whole lot of reasons for you to marry me but not the right one. Because I was being stalked—it seemed to me you even went out of your way to solve that problem so you could set me free with no guilt when the time came.'

'No, I didn't, Fleur,' he denied. 'I did it for two reasons. Because no one should have to live with that kind of fear or feel dependent on a ''protector'' forever. And because it goes against the grain with me to turn a blind eye to that kind of obsession or perversion.' He paused, and looked out to sea. 'The strange thing is, I thought that was why you married me.'

She swallowed as his gaze came back to her, and he smiled, a very faint echo of the old Bryn. 'But I didn't want you to feel grateful to me, in other words. I wanted there to be only one reason for you to be with me.'

It trembled on her lips to tell him his ego was showing but there were still shadows on her mind.

'Tom,' she said. 'I...'

'Tom,' he broke in gently, 'is going to be fine. And a lot of it is thanks to you. He accepted your departure quite equitably, not that he knew it was intended to be permanent. But he told Alana you needed to be with your mum for a while. And he told her that, at the same time, he was rather happy to have his very own mum because he was starting to like her very much but it had also been getting complicated at school, explaining to his friends who we all were.'

Fleur began to smile although with tears trickling

down her cheeks. 'He's such…such a character!' she said fervently. 'I'm so very happy for him. But I think what has helped Tom most through all this is that he's always been *loved*, even though people have come and gone in his life. And for that, you have to take a lion's share of the credit, Bryn.'

'Thank you,' he said, after a long, long moment when they'd stared at each other wordlessly. 'Could we talk about us? I mean, have I cleared the decks at all, Fleur?'

She gripped her hands. 'There's one other thing, Bryn. Did I…come into your life when you were discovering that Clam Cove was losing its appeal?'

He sat back and sighed. 'Not Clam Cove itself, ever. But I was beginning to need some new challenges and I was concerned about what my father was going through.' He paused and frowned. 'What are you trying to imply, Fleur?'

'I…it occurred to me you might have been looking for a diversion.'

He thought his way around this one for a long moment. Then he said simply, 'No. I just need you with me forever.'

'How will you cope with the head-turning bit?'

'By reminding myself of how terrible I felt when I knew I'd driven you away.'

'Did you?' she asked softly.

'Worse than I've ever felt in my life.' He looked at her and she saw the shudder that ran through him.

Her eyes widened.

'You said,' his gaze had never been more probing, or sombre at the same time, 'you'd cut all the ties. Was that true?'

She moistened her lips. 'I came back here because I

couldn't help myself, Bryn. I told myself it was to get
my things but then I found it was to…get some an-
swers. Why had it all gone so wrong?' She stopped
and looked at him with her heart in her eyes. 'I came
to the conclusion you were a falling star I would never
be able to catch, Bryn.'

'And now?' he said softly.

'There's just one question I can't seem to find the
answer to.' She paused and the tears started in her eyes
again and her voice was hoarse. 'How could you not
know…how deeply I'd fallen in love with you?'

He got up so swiftly his chair fell over. 'Because
I'm the most incredible fool,' he said roughly. Then
she was in his arms and he was holding her so hard
she could barely breathe. 'Do you really mean that?'
he said into her hair.

'Yes,' she breathed. 'Oh, yes.'

He took her to their bungalow and told her she'd never
been more beautiful as he unwound her sarong and
helped her out of her bikini. Then he laid her on their
bed to once again watch the sunlight and shadows playing over her body before he made love to her in a way
that was so very special that she was transported to
another world. A world that would always have at its
core for her this man….

They ran into the sea afterwards, joyfully naked.

He told her that if she loved Clam Cove so much,
they would never part with it.

She told him that it made her very happy to hear it
but had he made any decisions about what he wanted
to do with his life?

They were sitting on the beach, on their log, during
this conversation. He had cooked dinner and she had

made a lemon meringue pie to follow it. They'd opened a bottle of wine, and were finishing it as they sat beneath the stars.

'I...' he said slowly '...my father and I have agreed to sell out.'

'Oh, Bryn,' she murmured, looking at him with a touch of concern. 'Wouldn't that break his heart?'

'Strangely enough, no. It's getting harder and harder to survive the impact of multinational hotel chains and just before his operation he received an offer from one such chain. It's a good offer and they've guaranteed to keep the names of the hotels with theirs added. It's still the end of an era for the Wallis family.' He shrugged. 'Although, perhaps, the start of another one.'

'So you couldn't see yourself taking over from him?'

'No,' he said, quite definitely. 'It never was me, it never will be. Not on that scale. And I think that now we're all back together, Alana as well, he's finally come to understand and accept it. As a matter of fact, he looks years younger.'

'And you?' she queried.

He sipped his wine then studied the glass. 'One other thing made itself clear to me when I was going through hell thinking I'd lost you for good and by my own hand. I wasn't restless with Clam Cove, I was restless with myself.'

'You want to go back to being a war correspondent?' she asked and her eyes were suddenly fearful.

'No, never.' He put an arm round her shoulders and kissed the top of her head. 'But I think it's in my nature to be...possibly interfering, nosy and all the rest. Perhaps it's even in my nature to think I can put things right. I want to go back to journalism but in the form of picking a subject that really bugs me then writing the definitive series of articles about it. A lot of things do bug me. But that means travelling— You're laughing!' he accused.

'Oh, Bryn,' she laid her head on his shoulder, 'I love you.'

'Thank heavens,' he said devoutly. 'May I continue without being laughed at?'

'Please do,' she invited, although she was still smiling.

'In between travelling, with you, of course, I would love to come home to Clam Cove, with you. How does that sound?'

'It sounds wonderful. Could I be your research assistant?'

'With pleasure!'

'But...will we close down the restaurant permanently?' she asked.

'It's been suggested,' he said with surprising diffidence, 'that we make it into a family enterprise.'

Fleur sat up. 'You mean your father and Alana?'

'You don't mind?'

'No! I think that's brilliant. Are they really keen to do it, though?'

He grimaced. 'My father is champing at the bit. Alana is very keen and of course Tom is delighted at the prospect. There will always be times when we'd have the place to ourselves, though. I don't think Dad could adapt to the summers, although they're not as bad right here because we get the northerlies, when they blow. By the way—'

'The summers here at Clam Cove are the least of my worries, Bryn,' she broke in.

He hugged her. 'I was going to say that Julene and

Eric are happy to stay on, for a time anyway, so it won't be a case of dumping Dad, Tom and Alana here while we swan around the world finding causes to fight.'

'There may be times when I won't be able to swan around the world with you finding causes,' Fleur pointed out.

'Such as?' It was the old, autocratic Bryn who looked down at her with a frown.

'Well, I'm not sure about six kids but a couple would be nice,' she teased.

'I see. Of course. Well, we'll have to come up with a plan of action!'

She eyed him suspiciously. 'For having them or—?'

'Definitely. I like the sound of that very much, Mrs Wallis, and there's no time like the present!'

'Bryn, I didn't mean right away—'

'Not even a training session?' he broke in with the most wicked little smile playing on his lips.

'Perhaps,' she conceded. 'Although we had one not that long ago.'

'Practice makes perfect, isn't that what they say?'

'They might but—Bryn, I'm not going to bed with you until we discuss this properly,' she warned.

'I see. My wife has come up with a new set of guidelines,' he confided to the stars. 'I shall have to watch my Ps and Qs.'

Fleur sighed. 'Seriously,' she said, although she was trying not to laugh.

But all of a sudden he sobered. 'Fleur, seriously, we can plan and it may work out the way we plan. On the other hand, things may change—who knows? But I'm just as happy to have six kids as you are, if that's what's ordained for us, and to adjust our lives accordingly. There's one master plan, though, that will never change.'

'Tell me?' she said softly.

'You will always be the mermaid who sings to my soul, the siren I keep coming back to. Now that we've found each other—where, how, why—all those things will fall into place, don't you think?'

She trembled as he put his arms around her and thought of him sensing she was at Clam Cove, of everything that went to make up Bryn Wallis...

'I do,' she said against the corner of his mouth, 'my very own falling star.'

Modern Romance™
...seduction and
passion guaranteed

Tender Romance™
...love affairs that
last a lifetime

Sensual Romance™
...sassy, sexy and
seductive

Blaze.
...sultry days and
steamy nights

Medical Romance™
...medical drama on
the pulse

Historical Romance™
...rich, vivid and
passionate

29 new titles every month.

*With all kinds of Romance for
every kind of mood...*

MILLS & BOON®

Makes any time special™   MAT4

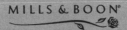

MILLS & BOON®

Modern Romance™

THE CITY-GIRL BRIDE by Penny Jordan

When elegant city girl Maggie Russell is caught in a country flood, rugged Finn Gordon comes to her rescue. He takes her to his farmhouse, laughs at her impractical designer clothes—and removes them piece by piece...

THE HUSBAND TEST by Helen Bianchin

Katrina has tried to forget she's still married to Nicos Kasoulis ever since she became convinced he was having an affair. Now, months later, Katrina has discovered that she can only gain control of her family business if she's reconciled with Nicos...for one year!

THE ITALIAN'S RUNAWAY BRIDE by Jacqueline Baird

When Kelly heard that her new husband Gianfranco didn't want *her* at all—just her baby, she had no choice but to run away. However, one thing was certain: Gianfranco would come after her...

LEGALLY HIS by Catherine George

Sophie's friends can't understand why she doesn't succumb to Jago Smith's seductive charm, but Sophie has very good reason not to: he is the barrister who failed to save her brother from a prison sentence...

On sale 7th December 2001

Available at most branches of WH Smith, Tesco, Martins, Borders, Eason, Sainsbury's and most good paperback bookshops.

1101/01a

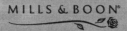

MILLS & BOON

Christmas
with a Latin Lover

Three brand-new stories

Lynne Graham
Penny Jordan
Lucy Gordon

Published 19th October

*Available at most branches of WH Smith,
Tesco, Martins, Borders, Eason, Sainsbury's,
and most good paperback bookshops.*

The perfect gift this Christmas from

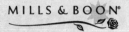

MILLS & BOON

*3 brand new romance novels and a
FREE French manicure set*

for just £7.99

featuring best selling authors
Betty Neels,
Kim Lawrence and Nicola Cornick

Available from 19th October

4 Books
and a surprise gift!

We would like to take this opportunity to thank you for reading this Mills & Boon® book by offering you the chance to take FOUR more specially selected titles from the Modern Romance™ series absolutely FREE! We're also making this offer to introduce you to the benefits of the Reader Service™—

- ★ FREE home delivery
- ★ FREE gifts and competitions
- ★ FREE monthly Newsletter
- ★ Books available before they're in the shops
- ★ Exclusive Reader Service discounts

Accepting these FREE books and gift places you under no obligation to buy; you may cancel at any time, even after receiving your free shipment. Simply complete your details below and return the entire page to the address below. *You don't even need a stamp!*

YES! Please send me 4 free Modern Romance books and a surprise gift. I understand that unless you hear from me, I will receive 6 superb new titles every month for just £2.49 each, postage and packing free. I am under no obligation to purchase any books and may cancel my subscription at any time. The free books and gift will be mine to keep in any case.

P1ZEB

Ms/Mrs/Miss/Mr ....Initials...
BLOCK CAPITALS PLEASE

Surname..

Address...

....

....Postcode ....

Send this whole page to:
UK: The Reader Service, FREEPOST CN81, Croydon, CR9 3WZ
EIRE: The Reader Service, PO Box 4546, Kilcock, County Kildare (stamp required)

Offer not valid to current Reader Service subscribers to this series. We reserve the right to refuse an application and applicants must be aged 18 years or over. Only one application per household. Terms and prices subject to change without notice. Offer expires 31st May 2002. As a result of this application, you may receive offers from other carefully selected companies. If you would prefer not to share in this opportunity please write to The Data Manager at the address above.

Mills & Boon® is a registered trademark owned by Harlequin Mills & Boon Limited.
Modern Romance™ is being used as a trademark.